AWESOME ADVENTURES OF FRANKIE STARGAZER

Josie A. Butler

PublishAmerica
Baltimore

First printing

ISBN: 1-60441-527-4
PUBLISHED BY PUBLISHAMERICA, LLLP
www.publishamerica.com
Baltimore

Printed in the United States of America

This book is dedicated to the memory of my husband and my hero, Frank (Jack) Butler, a firefighter who lost his life in the line of duty and to my children, grandchildren and great grandchild.

ACKNOWLEDGMENTS

I wish to acknowledge and give Glory, and Honor, and Thanksgiving to the Awesome God Almighty, Jesus Christ, King of Kings and Lord of Lords. Jesus is the Savior of the world, who gave his life for all mankind. Praise and worship God for who he is, for all he did, and for all he does for his children, and for his loving-kindness, and forgiving mercy.

God Bless my family, friends and Publish America for publishing the first true story I ever wrote titled, "Heart Of A Victim In Harm's Way and Beyond The Kissing Door."

I couldn't have continued to write without the support of my children, Joe, Greg, Angela and Frankie and their spouse's, Richard, Shelly and Renee. And to my grandchildren, Megan & Chris Roberts, Shane, Drenda, Chance, Joshua, Justin, Jonah and Jessie, and to my great grandchild, Tobey Matthew.

I'd like to thank my friends Soni, Denise, Gail, Sandy, Cindy Elder and Dr. Jirovec. Thanks to Jamie and Lonnie Senstock, aka, actor Ja'le Youngblood, Chance Williams, Lew and Pam Hunter, Mike Scanlan, Brad and Peg. Along with Screenwriter Chuck and Mary Jo Conaway, actress Lydia Cornell, actor Andrew Keegan and director Rob Walker. I'd like to thank Dori U, and my Angelo family, along with my new friends, Lauree, Helen, Vicki, Carol, Jody, Janet, Mosheen, Lori, David, Angie, Anne, Shauna, Guila , Linda, Terry, the nuns and the entire staff at Saint Elizabeth Regional Medical Center for the wonderful care they gave me while I was undergoing cancer treatment. A special thanks to my doctors, Richard Jirovec, Madhu V. Midathada, Dr. Wiltfong, Dr. Miller and to the doctors and staff in Radiology. I and my family are cancer survivors. Thank you Jesus.

TABLE of CONTENTS

INTRODUCTION

Proverbs...Chapter 24...Verse19...Do not fret because of evildoers, or be envious of the wicked; for there will be no future for the evil man; the lamp of the wicked will be put out.

Born with a purpose. Frankie Stargazer is a definitive force fighter predestined to fight crime and evil forces in adventurous situations, lined with diverse twists and events.

The story is intertwined with family values, interaction and romance.

One day Frankie has an accident and he slips into a coma. While he's unconscious, he is led down a path. It's made of liquid gold to a radiantly brilliant rainbow colored star. Where the voice of an invisible force, named "IAM informs Frankie that he is destined to accomplish unbelievable feats.

Awesome Adventures of Frankie Stargazer attracts attention to the battles that take place between the forces of good and evil.

CHAPTER 1 ...
THE FALLING STAR AND THE DREAM

For the eyes of the Lord move to and fro throughout the earth that he may strongly support those whose heart is completely his. The answer to evil will elude the wicked.

How could anyone know Frankie had a destiny that would change the course of his life? Out of all the humans, he alone was chosen to carry out daring, awesome feats as the most powerful force fighter of the Universe. There was no way of fathoming the incredible phenomenon's that were about to happen. My name is Joe. These were my thoughts as I watched my brother, Frankie, striding toward me. Before today, I had never noticed such gracefulness in the way he walked. Each stride gave his hair a subtle bounce that displayed beautiful, golden highlights glistening in the sun.

As he moved closer, there was a dazzling, sparkling twinkle in his blue eyes. It seemed as if the sun reflected in them, a brilliant star hidden deep in the recesses of each iris. The star was comparable to a slightly visible, thin white line, similar to the Lindsey star that shone within a particular blue sapphire stone.

There were times I simply thought of him as my pesky little brother who was forever getting in trouble, especially when he chose to skip school to go fishing. However, no matter what Frankie did, there always seemed to be an air of innocence about him.

As long as I live, the day Frankie was born will forever be etched in the recess of my being. There was a booming, thunderous lightning storm. It was like no other storm I ever witnessed. Wind whipped through the trees, as loud rumbling thunder roared overhead. I thought my eyes were playing tricks as a tremendous lightning bolt lit the dark night, like a flaming sword cutting through the sky. I swore I could faintly see the outline of an enormous bird, flying to and fro, but I surmised no human or animal could survive the outburst erupting outside.

From that day on, every time I saw a storm coming up on the horizon, I ran to the window to see if the sky had the same luminosity, flashing in the same manner it did the night Frankie was born. No storm ever compared with the dark, windy, noisy, light show I viewed that September evening. Sometimes, simply looking at Frankie gave me flashbacks to the eve he was born.

Frankie had traits that resembled the rest of the family but I must confess that the first time I saw him as a tiny baby, there seemed to be something different about him. Along with his stunning blonde hair and sparkling blue eyes, he had a smiling bubbly personality the second he took his first breath of air. His stunning smile could light up a room.

He had an unending, amount of energy. He liked to show off and let everyone see that he could do whatever he set his mind to. As he grew older, he continually repeated his own personal motto, 'If I can't do it, it can't be done.'

As I stood enjoying the day, I couldn't help thinking of the way he loved to tease and play tricks on his fellow classmates. I'm sure none of his teachers will ever forget the day Frankie caught a small, harmless snake, several frogs, and a dozen or so grasshoppers. He put them in a jar, hid them in his jacket, and took them to school. Shortly before school recess, he dumped the assortment of insects and amphibians out of the jar into the girl's bathroom. When the recess bell rang, the girls rushed in to use the restroom and came running right back out. They were screaming so loud, you could hear them throughout the entire school and possibly in China too!

My thoughts soon faded into the distance as Frankie approached me and said, "Hey Joe, What are you doing? Let's go to the park and play catch."

one, not even the doctors or nurses, could figure out where the luminosity was coming from. He still had a pulse and respirations, but Frankie was not responding.

Later on, Frankie told us that when he was in a coma he felt as if he was no longer in his body, lying so very still in the sterile hospital bed. Nor was he anywhere in the room, as the family solemnly stood praying by his bedside. He said he had the strangest dream. He was off in the distance, walking down a path, through a mist that looked like refined, liquid gold. He couldn't see or make out a figure, but he knew someone was holding his hand. It felt warm and comforting. An energized strength came over him as they continued striding toward colored lights shining brightly at the end of the path.

He finally reached the destination to which he was seemingly being led. At this point, he could no longer feel the warmth of someone holding his hand. Gazing at his surroundings, he felt alone and bewildered. He was standing in the midst of the most beautiful gold and white cloud, a star, or something. He wasn't quite sure what it was. There were stars everywhere. As he stood staring into space, another star suddenly appeared, casting-dazzling rainbow colors all around him. The colors seemed to be dancing in time to music. Abruptly, out of nowhere, he heard a voice that sounded like soft, rippling, rushing waters.

Frankie jumped sky high when he heard the voice speak. But the voice was gentle and had the most soothing effect, he soon calmed down. The voice said, "Frankie, don't be alarmed, I want to talk with you. In a few moments, you will be back with your family. I transported you to 'Rainbow Star' to enlighten you on a destiny, concerning certain powers with which you were born. You have been chosen to accomplish awesome phenomena's long before you were formed in your mother's womb. You were brought forth into the world with a purpose and providence. You have a destiny that will astound all mankind.

"I created the beautiful beckoning, sparkling star that you seek in the night sky. Although you don't see the star all the time, it continually shines on every step you take, even in the light of day.

Others view a starlit night, and see the magnificence of the Universe, but they can't see the special star I made especially for you. You couldn't invent or fashion in your wildest dreams, the plans you have been predestined to fulfill.

"When you're older and the time is right, you can decide with your own free will if you want to proceed into the unknown future. Most important is the fact, that no one can force you to accept the abilities. The powers can fade away and disappear just like that. The gifts are powerful forces you can't begin to comprehend at this time.

"They are powers, you won't be able to use in any way to benefit yourself in material gain or for selfish motives. They can only be used to do good works for others. At the present time you're not old enough to know if you wish to proceed into the unknown future.

Eventually, I'll teach you to overcome fear of the awesome truth of all I shall require, relating to the many diverse situations taking place in the world. When earthly human feelings tell you that you're all alone, always remember, I will never leave or forsake you in any way.

"The commanding powerful force you've been endowed with will be used to fight the battles mankind faces and have not the wisdom or knowledge to understand what they are up against."

Looking puzzled, Frankie asked, "Sir, could you please let me see what you look like?"

The soothing voice replied, "No Frankie, I'm afraid you can't look at me face-to-face. As a human being you couldn't survive seeing me. You must wait until you're ready to spend the remainder of eternity in my presence, before you can view my countenance."

Frankie didn't give up. He asked the voice once again, "If you won't let me see you, can you at least tell me who you are?"

"No son, not at this time."

Frankie said, "I'm so young! What can I possibly do to help anyone? I haven't even graduated from grade school yet."

The voice replied, "Don't be perplexed child. Many children were destined to do great things when they were your age and some were younger. When the time comes, I'll show you how to use the power force on enemies that attack and consume the hearts of people on planet earth. The abilities have a purpose, that will demonstrate that showing love and mercy can and will overcome the worst possible corrupt wickedness and evil.

"The supremacy of your feats will be revealed to only a handful of people. For no man is an island unto themselves. I'm aware of human nature's need to have someone they can relate to. When the chosen elect disclose certain truths, there will be no doubt in your mind, that I've allowed them to be a part of the new life force you're about to embark on."

Frankie said, "Sir, I remember the exact night the star fell and the way it suddenly landed in the spot it never wavers from. The second it gets dark outside, I run out to see if I can view the vividly brilliant star twinkling in the sky. Somehow, I just knew it was sparkling just for me. Sometimes, I anticipated the dazzling brilliance saying, "Hey there, Frankie, I see you laying on the roof." I wondered how something so fabulous and magnificent could shine down on me, when I'm just an insignificant speck sitting on a rooftop. I couldn't tell my family or friends all the things I imagined was happening. Whenever I ask anyone if they could see that one particular radiant star; they said that I just made it up and that I'm too much of a dreamer. After awhile I was careful who I talked to about the stars, or the way I wanted to fly around in outer space and explore the planets. I don't want anyone to tease me anymore than they already do."

The voice replied, "I've known you for a long time. I've seen all you have done from the time you were born. I noticed you on the roof night after night. It put a smile on my face to see the way you snuggle up to your dog, with her tail wagging outside of the blanket. I've watched as you gently reach over, and pull her tail back in under the covers, trying to keep her warm. A second later your dog's tail pops back out into the night air again.

"I've seen you doing the simplest chore and when you're walking and whistling down the street kicking a can. I see you all the time, wherever you are and whatever you do."

Frankie said, "I'd like to give my answer now sir or whoever you are. If you think I can do what you're asking of me then I'll do it. But golly, you're going to have to show me. I don't know how to do to many things. All I do now are my chores, play and go to school."

The voice calmly spoke, "Hush now Frankie. At this point in time I'm sending you back. You'll learn soon enough the things that will be required of you. In the meantime learn to do all things with love, compassion and kindness. Only then, will I begin to show you the mighty authority you've been gifted with, to overcome forces of pestilence and evil lurking through out the entire planet earth. I'm aware that you love space adventure. You're going to be privileged to see breathtaking wonders hovering in the vast universe, long before they are exposed by technology to future generations.

"That's enough for now. You learn more in the course of due time. I'm sending you back to your family now. It's time to wipe the sadness from their eyes and turn their worries into relief and joy."

Zoom!!! Boom!!! In the blink of an eye, Frankie was back in the hospital room. The glow that surrounded his bed mysteriously disappeared the instant he opened his eyes. The first words he spoke were, "Mom, Dad, I'm awake. I'm okay."

As the shock of hearing Frankie speak wore off, his parents said, "Thank God, son we were so worried. How do you feel?"

Frankie said, "I feel fine, I've been dreaming. I'm one powerful hungry boy."

Everyone laughed and talked at once. They couldn't stop hugging him. However, It was a few more days before he was released from the hospital.

Friends, neighbors and his dog, Kylee, were all waiting to greet him when he finally arrived home. Kylee was so happy to see Frankie; she leaped in the air and jumped smack dab into his open arms. Almost knocking him over, the dog wouldn't stop licking his face.

The glad tidings of welcoming Frankie home finally settled down. When the last guest went home, Frankie asked his family to gather around him. He tried to tell us about the dream he experienced in the hospital but Mom and Dad shushed him. Mom said, "Today was a big day. We can talk about your dream another time. The doctor explained, that you were not to have too much excitement. You need to rest."

Despite our parents' wishes for him to calm down, Frankie continued talking. He wanted his family to listen to the entire episode. His words ran one into the other as he tried to describe the way he stood in the midst of a cloud. He tried to explain the animation of radiant rainbow colors dancing in the middle of the bright golden star, and the voice that spoke to him. You could hear a pin drop as he tried to share his experience. We quietly stared at him with looks of pity.

After we listened to Frankie's story a few more minutes, Dad said, "Okay that's enough for tonight, son. Just sit back and relax a while. We are so thankful to have you home we don't want you to exert yourself in any way. The story your trying to tell us seems to be agitating your peace of mind."

Frankie looked helpless and weary. Needless to say, he was disappointed that he never quite finished sharing his story.

I knew just how to get Frankie's mind on other things. "Frankie do you remember the time you told your friends that you could swing through the tree tops like Tarzan the jungle man? They started taunting you to prove it and you led them to a certain area in the woods where the tallest trees grew wild. There were branches growing every which way among the thick foliage, where the sun didn't shine through the vast thickness of greenery. You climbed the tallest tree you could find while your friends jeered and cheered you on. You gave a wild hooting call, and started swinging from limb to limb. One of the branches hit you in the head and you fell to the ground and got right back up and said, 'I'm okay,' and then, you climbed right back up the tree again. You swung in the treetops until you were good and ready to climb down, unscathed. During the time you were whooping and hollering in the treetops, one couldn't help notice little critters living in hollowed out holes in the tree trunk peek out of their hiding places, unafraid, as they watched you perform in their territory. It was remarkable.

"It's always fascinated me to see the way animals show absolutely no fear of you. Like the time you were only five years old and you didn't tell anyone you were going to the park to play. You fell off the jungle gym, sprained your ankle and were unable to stand up and walk. Several hours went by before anyone realized you weren't around the house. The entire family took off in different directions to look for you. I ran to the park, and spotted you sitting in the middle of a dirt pile, under the jungle gym.

"There were squirrels, rabbits and birds sitting all around you. As I came closer to the unusual scene, I stood behind one of the huge oak trees, observing several tiny birds taking their little beaks and putting them in your mouth. It was so darn cute. It looked as if the birds were kissing you. Later on you told me that the birds were feeding you drops of water they carried in their little beaks from a flowing faucet located on the other end of the park.

Many is the time I've seen birds fly out of nowhere, land on your shoulder, and make cooing noises and then, they act as if they know what your saying when you gibber back to them.

"I have to admit, that particular scene in the park took my breath away. I stepped out from behind the tree, and the animals hurriedly scampered away the moment you hollered, 'Hey Joe! Am I ever glad to see you! I think I sprained my ankle. I'm having a hard time trying to stand up.' Then, I told you, 'Stay put. Don't try to move Frankie. I'll go get some help.'

You acted as if it wasn't unusual for the little animals to surround you in you're time of need. I don't know why but as I ran home, picturing the way you were laying on the ground with the little critters all around you, I thought of the ancient legend grandfather told us.

"Do you remember the story? It's the one about the legend that tells of a general whose army was afraid to fight. The soldiers were frightened because the enemy was too strong. Its fortress was too high and weapons too mighty. The king, however, was not afraid because he knew his men would win. How could he convince them? He had an idea so he told his soldiers he had a prophetic coin, which would foretell the outcome of the battle. On one side was an eagle, and on the other side, was a bear. He would toss the coin in the air. If it landed eagle side up, they would win. If it landed with the bear side up, they would lose.

"The army was silent as the coin flipped through the air. The soldiers held their breath as it fell to the ground. When they looked down at the coin, they shouted wildly because they saw the imprint of the eagle.

Bolstered by the assurance of victory, the men marched against the enemy and won. It was only after the victory, the king showed the men the coin. The two sides were identical, having an eagle on both sides.

I paused and looked at Frankie, "For reasons unknown to me, sometimes you remind me of an eagle soaring in the wind." Later, in the course of events, I reminded of the legend once again.

Frankie said, "Yes, Joe, I remember. But what does all that have to do with anything? I'm trying to tell you all about a new experience I had and no one wants to listen."

"It's not that we don't want to listen," I told him. "We just feel you should rest and try not to excite yourself. You don't have all your strength back yet. You gave us such a scare. At one point we thought you were a goner and we'd never see your blue eyes open again. Besides, I want you to know I've always thought that you are unique and have such special qualities unlike anything I've ever seen."

Frankie sat quietly as he contemplated my words. Meanwhile, I was back in my own thoughts. Little did I know the impact of my thoughts or the effect they would have later on.

Just then, Dad broke the silence and said, "Well, now that things have quieted down, I say we all retire to our rooms. Tomorrow is a new day and will be here soon enough."

We all said goodnight. Dad carried Frankie to his room and after tucking him in and saying a quick prayer, he went back down stairs to see how Mom was faring after the excitement of the day.

I'm the first child born to Jack and Mary Stargazer. Then there is Greg, Frankie, Angela and Lynn. Grandma and Grandpa Stargazer lived close by so we had the benefit of learning the older generation's wisdom too. We were showered with love. It felt as if we had the covering of a big umbrella over our entire family. It made us feel like we had a safety net around us at all times. I was once told that if there were holes in the unity of a family umbrella, anything could filter through the holes and take away the net of protection that shields a family from outside influences. It was great to belong to a family that had binding ties to one another.

As children, we still had our share of arguments and squabbles. We debated endlessly, as to who was the toughest child. But overall, we felt protected, as though nothing could harm or touch our little piece of the world.

CHAPTER 2…
AWESOME POWERS BEGIN TO EMERGE

The moment Frankie woke up on his first morning home from the hospital, he went outdoors to see if everything was still intact. He wanted to make sure his playthings were just the way he left them.

As he stood outside enjoying the morning sunshine, he swore, he heard, music playing in the wind. As the wind blew gently through the treetops, he noticed the leaves flowing back and forth. The leaves and every tiny blade of grass essentially looked as if they were keeping time to the melody. He shook his head, thinking he could shake the sound away. But the music continued to play. It was like nothing he had ever seen or heard before.

He didn't know what to think. He stood there listening to the beautiful music. He couldn't pinpoint the type of instruments, he was hearing. It felt as if he could reach out and touch the wind. Each time he put his hand up in the air, the melody changed to a different tune.

The music didn't seem to have a set timing; it simply surged forth and flowed with each gush of wind. He stuck his head in the house to see if someone had turned on the radio. The only thing he heard were the sounds of his family getting ready for school. The melody definitely wasn't coming from inside the house.

Looking all around, he tried to figure out what the heck was going on. Frankie had the strangest feeling that someone was watching him. Unpredictably, he glanced up at the sky and nearly jumped out of his skin. He saw an eagle big as a mountain hovering high in the air. It was pure grandeur, with majestic colors of brown, gold and white. The eagle's wings were spread out, but it wasn't flying. It simply stayed stationary, directly above him and it only moved, when he did. He felt as if the humongous eagle was keeping him under the cover of its wings on purpose.

Frankie thought 'Holy bazooka!' Maybe the accident affected his vision and that he might be hallucinating. Or else, he was merely dreaming and walking in his sleep. It just couldn't be real.

Just about the time he felt as if he were going to faint, he heard his Mom calling. By this time, Frankie couldn't move. He just stood mesmerized. When Mom didn't hear him answer, she opened the door and walked outside and stood next to him. He looked at her to see what kind of reaction she was having to the panoramic view of all that was happening. To his amazement, Mom didn't acknowledge anything.

She merely said, "What are you doing up so early? Why are you standing outdoors in your pajamas? I told you, the doctor says you need to take it easy. You're not to get out of bed for a few more days."

A few seconds after Mom spoke, Frankie came back to reality. He was flushed and excited. He asked his Mom to look up at the sky. His words were so slurred and fast; she ignored what seemed to be more of his incomprehensible chatter.

When Frankie finally got his bearings back, he stuttered as he said, "For goodness sake, Mom, can't you hear the music?"

She looked at him with sympathy, concerned that he was still shaken from the accident. She wasn't paying any attention to what she estimated to be another one of his fairytale's.

Frankie finally spoke more coherently. He said, "Mom, answer my question. Did you see the trees swaying to and fro or the giant eagle hovering in the sky?" As he waited for her reply, he noticed the look of disbelief on her face. The look that simply said, 'Oh dear, what am I going to do with this child?' He took that as a cue not to say anymore or she'd make him go in the house to rest. She probably wouldn't let him get out of his bed again, until he was eighty years old.

It was all so frustrating. More than anything, Frankie wanted his family to believe him. He was tired of them looking at him like he was fantasizing loony tunes. All he wanted was to run, jump and play. He wanted to be treated like he wasn't goofy from the blow on his head. But more than that, he wanted his family to acknowledge his words. After seeing the look of bewilderment on his mother's face, he knew it was futile to continue their conversation any further. He was a little confused when he walked into the house. Perhaps his family was right. Maybe, the blow on his head had affected him more than he wished to admit. He couldn't help thinking, 'For goodness sake, what in the world is happening?' The music had stopped as abruptly as it started. Turning to take one last glance up at the sky, he observed, that the eagle was no longer hovering overhead either.

Frankie trudged into the house. All he could think about was the strange vision he'd encountered that morning. How could it possibly be a dream when he was so wide-awake? He really had heard music in the wind and seen the trees and grass dancing. He just knew there was no way he could have imagined seeing the gigantic eagle.

At this point he wasn't sure who to confide in. He had to talk to someone that would listen. Someone that would believe he wasn't making it all up. Frankie contemplated telling his older brother. Joe was one of the few people that didn't get a funny look in his eyes like everyone else did when he tried to explain exciting incidents.

The dream, and the voice he heard while he was in a coma, and now all that he had encountered in his very own back yard was the first and the last thing he thought of when he woke up and when he went to bed. It was fantastically incredible!

In the meantime, he decided, he was just a twelve-year-old kid. All he wanted to do was play and frolic with his siblings and the neighbor children.

Frankie, had a lot of friends, but his very best friend was Sam. The two were inseparable. They spent every waking moment they could at each other's houses. Sam lived right next door to Frankie. Through the years they had their share of 'boys will be boys' escapades.

Just then, there was a knock on the door. It was Sam. Frankie was so glad to see him. Sam said, "Hey Frankie, how are you doing today? Feel any better?"

Frankie said, "Yes I do. What have you been up to?"

"Not much. I thought I'd come over and see what you were up to." Sam said.

Frankie replied, "Actually, I was just thinking about you."

Sam asked, "What about me?"

Frankie said, "I was trying to get my mind off things and I started to think about some of the ornery things we used to do. Like the times we used to sneak in the movie theater with the other kids when the usher's back was turned. And, the way everyone said the pranks you couldn't think of, I could."

Sam said, "Yeah. Remember that one Halloween night when we both got the same bright idea when that grumpy guy down the street was mean to us? We filled a paper bag full of dog doo, and then we put the sack on his porch, set it on fire, rang the doorbell, and ran. We hid in the bushes and watched him open the door and stomp on the burning sack. No need to guess what happened next, hey Frankie."

Frankie replied, "Yes I do and I recall the time we dared you to jump out of the top window of a two-story house. You had to show us you weren't chicken so you jumped. It didn't matter that you just had a hernia surgically removed a few months before. Luckily, you weren't hurt. Sam, you are always so adventuresome. You're a real daredevil.

"You had to overcome a lot of teasing from you're younger days. You used to be fearful every time a plane flew overhead, because you thought each one that you heard was a warplane, ready to bomb your territory. No matter where you were playing, the instant you heard a plane you'd run into the basement to hide. The kids in the neighborhood never let you forget it. They called you 'chicken little.' Needless to say, as you grew older, you'd do whatever it took to show that you were tough and was no longer afraid of airplanes or anything else that crossed your path."

Sam smiled, "Yeah, those were the good old days."

For a while both boys just sat quietly, staring into space identifying with some of the pranks they pulled.

As they sat silent in their own thoughts, Frankie was thinking about the way he related more to his friend Sam than to any of his other friends. Sam was a dreamer too. They both liked space, the stars and science fiction. Sam talked about flying to the moon and other planets. He commanded Frankie's undivided attention. Sam's ideas seemed mostly futuristic garble, yet Frankie was captivated. It seemed strange that there we're times Sam seemed to be talking about the same planets the voice spoke to him about in his fantastic prophetic dream.

However, at this point, Frankie still didn't feel comfortable telling Sam about his dream, the music in the wind or the gigantic eagle just in case his friend might think he was making it up in the same way they imagined and made things up about space travel. He didn't think he could take it if his best friend thought the same way others did. It had to be a time when Sam would accept that Frankie was telling him the absolute truth and not fantasy.

Other than his brother, Joe, Frankie was weary of telling anyone about his experiences since he had the accident. They treated him like he was a nut case. As a matter of fact, Frankie stopped trying to tell his mom and dad about the dream altogether because they continued pooh poohing his words as an illusion of his imagination.

Sam finally interrupted Frankie's thoughts by saying, "I have to go home and help my mom. I'll be back later."

Frankie said, "Okay. See you later alligator."

Frankie still wasn't certain what he experienced while he was in a coma, or on that first morning when he walked outdoors after he came home from the hospital. There were days he thought the dream seemed like it was a real true experience. But as time wore on, he didn't dwell on it as much as he used to.

In the meantime, as his older brother I couldn't help but secretly wonder about all the things Frankie told me about his experience in the hospital. Some of the tales he related made me question how my younger brother could possibly come up with such far-fetched stories. I tried to listen objectively to all the things Frankie said. But wow, the stories were far out. I surmised that Frankie's sagas were very real to him. Even though they were not real to anyone else.

Frankie knew someone else he recognized not just as a friend but also as an ally. She was someone he could turn to when all else failed. Her name was Cynthia. She lived directly across the street from the Stargazers. Cynthia had black hair and green eyes. She was very petite and slender. She never did grow taller than 5 feet. When she felt like it, she could be feisty. But mostly she was kind and gentle. They shared a lot of confidences with one another but at this point, he couldn't tell her about his latest secrets either.

During hot summer days after the chores were done, Frankie and Cynthia took lemonade and sandwiches to the park. They played until they wore themselves to a frazzle. Catching their breath, they laid on the grass under a tree, staring intently at the blue skies. The two imagined every shape and form they could think of, as the clouds rolled and tumbled in the sky, ever changing into different images. At times the clouds were so enormous and dazzling white, they looked like fluffy mounds of cotton, floating upward higher and higher in the air, reaching clear into the heavens.

It seemed as if the oak trees in the park were the tallest and the oldest trees in the world. They had the biggest, most beautiful leaves that flew majestically through the air, before they gently touched the ground. There were trees all around the park, but the majority of them covered the area where the play equipment was located. No matter how hot it was, the trees kept the play area cool.

Across the street from the park was the vicinity referred to as "The Woods." There was a long, winding path that cut through wild, untamed areas. At the end of the path, was a clearing and you could see the enormous red hills rising from the sandy banks of the river's edge. The landscape was breathtaking. It was peaceful the moment you caught a glimpse of the scenery beyond the jungle of trees and bushes. Fishing down by the river was one of the town's meeting places. It didn't matter what time of day it was, there always seemed to be someone with a fishing pole dangling in the water.

Every time we entered the woods we felt as wild as the animals, roaming in the tangled greenery, scurrying for shelter when they heard a noise. It never occurred to us to be frightened of the critters. We thought of them as our friends. We wanted to bring some of the critters home. Except, Dad thought every animal he saw had to be butchered and eaten.

Quite often Frankie had to baby-sit his youngest sister Lynn. She was a beautiful little girl with auburn hair and flashing brown eyes. Her personality was curious and easy going. Frankie often took her to play in the park. Lynn loved going places with her brother. He always held her hand and watched over her like he was afraid she'd break. He was gentle and tender with her. Most of all he wouldn't let anyone tease her. Those were lazy days, filled with fun times.

Lynn often said some of her fondest memories and best times were when Frankie took her fishing and let her frolic to and fro. He gave her as much time as she wanted to run up and down the beautiful red hills. Allowing her to feel free as a butterfly, dancing from flower to flower, while he tried to catch enough fish for supper. Mom was always tickled when he came in with a string of catfish.

Fishing and hunting wasn't just a luxury or a pastime. At times it was a matter of survival. The Stargazers, like most everyone else during the forty's lived off the fruit of the land. Along with fishing and hunting they gathered nuts and berries or whatever could be found in the woods to enhance mealtime. They had a huge garden. There were apple, pear, peach and cherry trees scattered around their huge backyard.

There were many days when neighbors shared a plate of cookies, a loaf of bread or a bountiful harvest of fruit and vegetables while trying to survive in an era that was still going through hard lean times.

The impending wars that rocked the country took its toll on the economy. Jobs were scarce, and people sacrificed, rationed, and did without some of the barest necessities.

A new pair of shoes was a major item in the family budget. Dad scrimped and saved every penny he could. By the time we did get a new pair of shoes, our old ones were threadbare. We wore those new shoes with such pride. We showed off, strutted around, and acted like they were the last pair of shoes in the whole world.

Regardless, time passed, as did the wars and the lean times. As we grew a little taller, and a little older, we enjoyed the kind of fun that goes hand in hand with living in a small town. On the other hand, simply because we lived in a small town, didn't mean we shouldn't be careful because our town had it's share of crime, prejudice, vandalism and gossip. Nothing escaped the wagging tongues of our tiny society. If a baby was born, or if someone passed away, the whole town knew about it before it hit the local news. It seemed like an invisible bulletin board went up every time a new family moved into the area.

One was considered elite if they had a new bike or owned toys that was bought in a store. Most of the toys we played with were homemade. Itching to make a pretend racecar, we haunted the alleys behind the grocery stores to pick up orange crates they had thrown in the trash pile.

Since Frankie and his friend, Sam talked endlessly about space and flying to the moon, they always made the crates into make believe rocket ships. The family once thought the reason Frankie liked swinging through the tree tops was connected to the dreams he had of flying through space, swinging on a star, and carrying moon beams home in a jar.

That's the way things were at this point in time and no one was the wiser. There was nothing we could do but to simply accept whatever the day offered good, bad or indifferent.

Besides, being creative wasn't a chore. It was fun! The sense of accomplishment, and the compliments from Mom and Dad made us feel

good. Our parents were never slow to tell us how proud they were when we did a good job. However, they never failed to tell us when we messed up either. Mom and Dad were two of the most kind-hearted people one could hope to know. They disciplined and punished us when we had it coming, but never harshly. It was always done in love.

One disciplinary action that took place after an incident that stands out was the day Frankie decided to bomb blast me with a water balloon. He knew I left the house at the same time each day to deliver newspapers. One morning, he waited for me to leave the house, contemplating the laugh he'd get throwing a water balloon on my head from the upstairs window the moment he heard me take a step out the back door.

Dad was running late for work. He rushed out the door and when Frankie heard the door open, he let loose of the water balloon and it splattered all over Dad, saturating every inch of his clothing with water. He wasn't happy about the shower he encountered as he stepped out the door. Frankie was grounded and had to stay in his room an entire week. Naturally, we always felt bad about misbehaving and upsetting our parents. Afterwards, we'd try harder than ever to please them.

Mom and Dad always said that as the oldest brother, I was considered to be sensible, with a quiet gentle manner. Therefore, Greg, Angela, Frankie and Lynn leaned heavily on me, while they revealed all their idiosyncrasies. I was their confidant, defender and righter of wrongs, during the arguments that sometimes flare up between brothers and sisters.

One of the things Lynn confided was that she couldn't understand why the experience Frankie had in the hospital was more like a premonition. As if someone was trying to tell him things he couldn't understand. She didn't exactly know what to think because Mom and Dad kept saying that Frankie was describing a delusion.

All she could think of during the time he was unconscious was that she was afraid he was never going to wake up again. Lynn was thrilled whenever her brothers told her any of their secrets. More than anything in the world, she loved her family and she wanted to be good friends with her brothers.

I advised Lynn not to take everything people said to her so seriously. But she continued to believe all that Frankie told her, for she knew he loved and protected her. No matter what kind of trouble he got into Frankie graciously accepted his punishment without uttering a word.

CHAPTER 3...
WINGS OF AN EAGLE

The family was planning a thirteenth birthday party for Frankie. Mom and Dad couldn't afford to have a birthday party for us every year. But they always let us have a party on the day we became a teen. They thought becoming a teenager was a big deal and a special occasion that called for a celebration, no matter how tight money was. It was such a happy, memorable time the memories and reminiscences would last a lifetime.

Frankie could hardly wait. The parties were planned to match a certain theme and we all dressed for the topic of the party. The entire family pitched in and decorated the back yard. The picnic table would be set with fresh squeezed lemonade, tiny sandwiches, potato salad, candy, cake and homemade ice cream.

We amused ourselves with made up games, played musical instruments and danced. All evening long, foot-stomping music floated through out the neighborhood. The family affair included Grandpa playing the fiddle and Grandma playing an accordion.

Excited about his upcoming party the day of Frankie's birthday finally arrived. The weather was unusually hot for September. When school was out, he ran all over looking for his friends but he couldn't find any of them. He finally gave up and hurried home without them. Sure enough, his friends had ditched him on purpose and they were already waiting at his house. The moment Frankie walked in the door, they all shouted, "Surprise!"

The theme of the party turned out to be the "Old Wild West' days. Everyone was dressed in homemade western attire. Frankie changed his clothes and the festivities started the minute he walked outside looking handsome and grown up in his homemade western outfit.

Since the next day was Saturday, Mom and Dad let us stay up a little later than they usually did. The birthday celebration lasted until eleven pm.

The party was a big hit not only with the Stargazers, but with the neighbors too. No one needed an invitation. When they heard the music and the laughter taking place in the Stargazer's back yard, they took it as a cue to join the celebration

After the party, Frankie walked Cynthia across the street to her house and he received his first kiss on the lips. He was in seventh heaven as he walked back across the street with his head in the clouds. When he came in the front door, we noticed his blue eyes were sparkling more than they usually did. He bid everyone goodnight, grabbed his bedding and climbed out the window to sleep on the roof, with his faithful friend, Kylee. Kylee was a rare breed of dog called a Chinese Sharpie. She was all wrinkly and crinkly. She was the most stunning chocolate colored puppy. Although the dog loved and played with the whole family, Kylee attached herself to Frankie. The dog rarely let him out of her sight. Frankie couldn't get up from a chair or walk from one room to the next without the dog following him every step of the way.

As Frankie lay on the roof contemplating the day's festivities, he noticed the bright star he kept his eye on each night seemed bigger and brighter than it usually did. He could see gold, red, violet, blue and green colors adorning the star. They were the same colors that surrounded and danced all around as the wonderful voice spoke to him almost a year ago. He thought the star looked especially remarkable. It was the end to a perfect day.

But the day wasn't over for Frankie. He was awakened in the middle of the night by the soft, rippling sound he had heard once before. The power in the speech hearkened Frankie to go to the highest point on the roof. He got up and obeyed the voice he recognized as being the same one he heard in his dream.

Frankie was still sleepy and groggy when he started climbing to the top of the roof; he stumbled, rolled off and was about to hit the dirt. Suddenly, his arms and hands flew straight outward away from his body and wings resembling an eagle unfolded. The mass of feathers started gliding Frankie upward. Before he knew what happened, he was soaring higher and higher.

Amazingly, Frankie wasn't afraid as the power to fly manifested. He simply thought he was having a whimsical fantasy. He was flying further and further away. He did loop da loops, laughing and playing in the black night sky, with the wings that had popped out of nowhere. It was as if he knew exactly how to use them to manipulate frolicking in the sky. The huge eagle Frankie had seen once before was gliding right above Frankie's head. He sensed the bird was watching over him. He felt certain if he had any trouble the giant eagle would swoop down beneath him and make sure no harm would befell him, in his newfound freedom in flight.

In what seemed like an instant, he found himself standing in the midst of the same 'Rainbow Star' he viewed once before. Immediately upon his arrival, the beautiful, soothing voice that greeted him when he was in a coma, greeted him once again.

The first thing the voice asked was, "How do you like flying?" The wings are merely one source of power that will automatically vanish as quickly as they appeared.

"The wings will manifest whenever you need to use them, plus any time you wish to fly simply for your own enjoyment. You must use wisdom and never abuse the force of abilities and powers that will soon be revealed to you. You have the ability to fly to any planet or star in the universe and there will be no problem breathing. The utmost reason you have the ability to fly is to help rescue those in need."

Frankie asked, "Am I dreaming?"

The stunning voice said, "No, you're not dreaming. All you've witnessed thus far is real. Don't fret if no one believes you. They're not aware of all the tasks and battles you're about to confront and endure. One more thing you need to be aware of before going back to your corner of the world, is that 'The Lindsey Star' that sparkles and lights up the iris's in your eyes has amazing great power within them.

"Your eyes will do feats that will surface and be apparent when you're fighting unseen shadows. In the space of time, one look and one quick turn will freeze everyone and everything around you. No one will remember anything that took place. With the blink of an eye everything you froze in time, will resume back to the same way it was before the encounter. There will be many diverse looks that will allow you to expedite different skills, as you need them. Each look will be different than the other.

"Diverse looks from your eyes will throw lightning bolts. Another look will apprehend evildoers, another, will put a wall of safety around whomever you're rescuing. There are too many force's and resources to learn in one lesson. You will become skilled with the capability to remember every gift you're endowed with. They will be a part of your being until your destiny is fulfilled.

"When we speak again, I'll teach you that every power has a purpose. I called you to visit the star on your special day to assure you that you're not dreaming. Nothing concerning my will for you or the planet earth is in your imagination.

"You may call me, "IAM." We can speak anytime, anywhere. I'll listen when you're puzzled, or in need of a friend, or have misgivings and problems that arise and captivate you. It may surprise you to know that your Grandfather and Grandmother have known about me for years and they believe I'm real. They're aware of some of the battles taking place in the supernatural realm.

"They don't speak of everything they've learned through the years. They have great wisdom and share only what they believe people can handle. In due time, I'll reveal some of your powers to your brother Joe, and Greg along with a few others.

"Frankie, I want you to understand you have the right to decide your own destiny. I will not be offended if you want to decline. All that has occurred thus far will be erased from your mind. At this time, I need to ask if you want to serve me?"

"Yes sir, I believe I do," Frankie said.

IAM asked, "Do you remember what I told you the first time we talked?"

Frankie replied, "Yes I do. I remember every word you spoke. But I've got to tell you; even though I pondered on all that happened and all you told me, I had my doubts. I began to believe that maybe everyone was right. Even though it seemed real, maybe I really did dream or imagine all that took place.

The voice said, "If at any time you decide you don't want to accept the challenge of the future and tackle the deeds set before you, simply call out the name, "IAM." I'll come to your rescue and you won't remember anything that happened up to that point. You've had enough excitement for one day. I'm sending you back home. We will be in touch again."

In the next instant Frankie was back on the roof sleeping. The dog hadn't budged an inch but when Kylee felt her master's warm body, she snuggled closer.

CHAPTER 4…
THE BRAVE RESCUE

When Frankie woke up the next morning he rushed into the bathroom to look at his body and examine his eyes. He didn't see anything unusual. His body and his eyes looked the same. Even though he couldn't grasp the full meaning of all that he experienced the night before, he knew without a shadow of a doubt that it was not a dream or a figment of his imagination. It was real.

Still, Frankie had his own thoughts. He couldn't help but wonder, why me? "Why didn't the awesome voice pick one of his brothers, or Sam, or for that matter anyone other than me?" He decided the next time he had the opportunity to talk to the voice of IAM, he'd ask him why, he was chosen to have a destiny that was to be so different from the rest of his family and friends? Then, Frankie thought, wow, not only my family, this could quite possibly mean he was chosen over every single person in the world.

He didn't know for sure who the voice of IAM belonged to. He just had to accept that IAM was a powerful force in the Universe. He was bursting to tell everyone, but he decided he'd better not tell anyone just yet. No one would believe him anyway. They would probably just think he was stranger than they already deduced. His parents might even take him to see the doctor again. Worse than taking him to see the doctor, they threatened to take him to a psychiatrist if he continued to talk about the star and the voice.

Frankie spoke aloud, "Okay, twinkle, twinkle little star, I won't tell a soul. I'll take it a day at a time. If I don't think I can handle the responsibility, I'll just say, I don't want a destiny or a purpose."

For the time being, he just wanted to be a teen-age boy, doing whatever his friends did.

Maybe later on, he could talk to Joe, or Cynthia, or Sam about his experiences. He just didn't know. He wasn't ready to make any decision yet, it's not like the world was going to end today.

Putting the events of the night aside, Frankie showered and ran downstairs. All his feelings went back to the fact that at long last, he was a teenager. He didn't feel any different but he couldn't wait to find out what his brothers meant when they kept telling him to wait until he was thirteen and he would see for himself that everything changes.

Frankie had plenty of changes but they had nothing to do with the things his brothers told him or with being a teen. If everything was as good as his first real kiss, he couldn't wait to see what was next.

After he showered and dressed, he went next door to pick Cynthia up and walk to school together. She wasn't home so he proceeded to Sam's house to see if he was ready. Sam was having breakfast so Frankie sat down at the kitchen table with him and had a bite to eat too.

On the way to school, Sam talked about spaceships and what they would do if they saw space invaders in their back yard. Before they knew it, they were standing by the front door of the school.

With a mischievous look in his eye, Sam said, "Let's play hooky and mess around down by the river."

Frankie replied, "I don't know if we should skip school today. I don't want to get in trouble after the nice party my parents gave me last night."

It didn't take much coaxing to sway Frankie and before he knew it they were running towards the woods. They hid their books by a big stone and scattered leaves all around to hide them. Singing and cutting up they took their sack lunch with them and walked down to the river.

Frankie and Sam had a stash by the river where they kept a knife, a ball of string and fishhooks. They cut a couple tree branches, tied the string and hooks on the branch and Walla, they had a fishing pole. They hunted for bugs and worms. Before long the boys were laying on a rock, near the water, fishing with the handmade poles. Apprehension over skipping school went by the wayside.

As Sam and Frankie were whiling away the day, a loud voice pierced the stillness. Someone was hollering for help. Startled, they jumped up and climbed up on a rock to see if they could see where the voice came from. Lo and behold, there was a man in the middle of the river down stream splashing, gurgling and hollering for help. It looked as though he might have fallen off a big tree partially lodged in the river. Frankie and Sam were the only other people around. As they started to run by the riverbank toward the man, he went under the water.

Frankie couldn't exactly explain what happened next. When he saw the river water rippling around the man's sinking body, all he could think of in that moment was saving him. He ran like a gazelle, leaving Sam in a cloud of dust. He jumped so high; he landed halfway across the river, right next to the drowning man. He went under the rippling river water and saw the man's foot was tangled in a rope that was caught on something deep down in the water.

Frankie's eyes zapped the rope in half. He grabbed the man and in an instant they bolted to the surface. Sam stood by the edge of the river with his mouth wide open, waiting as Frankie swam toward him holding onto the drowning man. Sam helped yank the man out of the water and placed him safely on the sandy banks.

After a few minutes of applying resuscitation, the man started coughing. He spit up the river water he'd swallowed. Although he was quite shaken, he was breathing normally again. He sat up; dazed at first, then as the boys came into focus, he repeatedly told them how grateful he was that they were close by.

He wanted to know their names so he could reward them, but the boys said, "No, it's okay. We are glad we we're here to help. We really don't want anything."

They were hesitant to tell the man their names for fear they'd get in trouble for skipping school. The man said he couldn't thank the boys properly if he didn't know who they were. Sam and Frankie were really shaken up. They tried to act calm, but they ended up telling the man their names.

They walked the man up the hill and helped him get into his car. He told them his name was Mr. Walters. He thanked them again, started his car and with a wave of his hand, he drove off down the winding dirt road. Frankie and Sam both figured they'd never see him again so they wouldn't have to worry about anyone finding out they played hooky.

The actions Frankie undertook in the rescue not only took Sam by surprise, they took him by surprise too.

Frankie tried to explain to his friend that he didn't do anything spectacular. The only thing that transpired was that his adrenalin reacted to someone in trouble. The boy's traipsed back to the spot where they left their fishing poles and ate their lunch. As they munched on peanut butter and jelly sandwiches, they both had their own thoughts swirling through their brain.

Subsequently, Sam said, "Frankie what's up? You've never won a race in your life. You couldn't even jump two inches at the track meet. I could hardly believe my eyes when you jumped halfway across the river. I just can't believe adrenalin could give you that kind of strength. Mr. Walters is twice your size and yet, you lugged him to the riverbank like he was a feather."

Frankie replied, "I don't have any answers. In my entire life I never did anything remotely close to all that occurred today. All I did was react to the situation and it gave me the potency to save the man's life. He contemplated Sam's words a few minutes, and then Frankie said, "I don't want to fish anymore, let's head for home."

"Golly, we can't go home yet. School won't be out for another two hours," Sam said.

Frankie remarked, "I'm soaking wet. Let's go somewhere. I've had enough excitement for one day."

They stashed their fishing gear and went to pick up the books they had stashed by the big gray rock. They decided to hide in the tree hut Joe and Greg built a few years ago until it was time to go in the house. It surely had to be a first that neither boy had anything to say as they walked home in silence.

Before they could climb into the safety of the tree house, Frankie's Grandpa happened to be close by. He noticed the boy's wet clothing as they were hiking up the ladder.

Grandpa called out, "What are you boys doing? Come on down here."

They scampered back down the rickety ladder leading to the tree hut. They both had a sheepish look on their face as Grandpa told them to come along with him. They walked across the street to Grandpa's house. The first thing he did was to tell the boys to take off their wet clothes, gave them a towel to cover themselves and threw the wet clothes on the line to dry in the warm sunshine.

The boy's confessed to playing hooky. Then they told Grandpa about the man that almost drowned. He listened intently and then said, "It was lucky for the man that you boys happened to be there.

Sam said, "The man's name is Mr. Walters."

Frankie could see a look of recognition come over Grandpa's face when he mentioned the name Walters so he asked, "Do you know him?"

Grandpa said, "Yes. I do know him. He's a prominent attorney and a very wealthy man. He inherited a fortune. He lives in that remodeled old mansion on the hill. It's one of the most beautiful places in town."

Grandpa wondered how Mr. Walters happened to be fishing on a workday and why he was alone? He never goes anywhere without his chauffer who also acted as his bodyguard. Grandpa contemplated the children's words a few moments, and then, he said, "Well, you children have certainly had an interesting day. You know you're going to have to tell your parents the events of the day. Although they'll be proud of your brave deed, they're not going to be too happy with either one of you for skipping school."

Frankie asked, "Grandpa can you come with us while we tell them?"

Gramps said, "I think it's best for both of you to fess up to all of it on your own. In the meantime, I'll get you some of Grandma's home baked cookies and a glass of ice-cold milk. Then you both better scamper home and face the music."

Frankie said, "Sam, I guess the best way to go about this is for both of us to face my mother first, then we'll go tell your Mom. Maybe our parents won't get too upset if we stick together."

They put their dried clothes back on, thanked Grandpa, took a deep breath and ambled over to Frankie's house first.

They walked in the back door and Frankie immediately called out, "Mom, I'm home, where are you?

She came up from the basement. She was surprised to see the boy's were home from school already.

Mom said, "Hi boys. Did school let out early?"

Frankie replied, "No Mom, we played hooky and something happened."

Mom exclaimed, "Oh my goodness, boys, what have you been up to?"

Frankie said, "We went fishing, a man was drowning and they rescued him and that's all there was to it, no big deal. We were afraid to go back to school and then we ran into Grandpa. He dried our clothes, gave us cookies and milk and here we are.

Mrs. Stargazer frowned as she said, "Frankie, you've just told me too little, too fast. I need details."

"Well, Mom. We made a couple of fishing poles and we were sitting on a rock by the river, when we heard a man calling for help. We ran and pulled him out of the river and gave him first aid. That's all there is to tell," Frankie replied.

Mom said, "Frankie, if this is true, I can't fault you for saving a soul, for that is no small feat and not to be treated lightly, but it doesn't take away from the fact that you played hooky again. How many times do we have to tell you how important school is? You need an education if you intend to get a good job some day. We have to tell your father as soon as he come's home from work. He's not going to be happy about this. Now tell me again, what happened."

Frankie and Sam blurted out the details once more.

Frankie said, "Could we go to Sam's house now to tell his parents?

Mom replied, "You're not going anywhere Frankie."

"Mom it's only fair both of us tell Sam's Mom in the same way we told you."

"Okay son, but you're to come straight home the minute you boys finish talking to Sam's mother."

The same scene took place at Sam's house. Afterwards, Frankie bid Sam farewell and went home to face the lecture he knew he was about to receive from both his parents.

The boys were praised for rescuing Mr. Walters, but needless to say, both of them were grounded for a month. They weren't even allowed to walk to school together for the same amount of time. That was punishment enough. Frankie and Sam had not gone more than a day without seeing one another. They were going to miss the camaraderie they shared daily.

As expected, after the month passed by, Frankie and Sam were back to being inseparable.

Several weeks after the grounding punishment was over a big fancy car driven by a chauffeur arrived at the Stargazer residence. A man, woman and the chauffeur walked to the door carrying several baskets of goodies. It was filled to the brim with staples of food. The baskets contained every kind of fruit, varieties of candy and nuts imaginable. It turned out to be Mr. Walters and his wife. He spoke to Mrs. Stargazer a few minutes and asked if he could speak to Frankie and his friend, along with Sam's folks too.

Frankie excitedly ran lickity split to fetch Sam and his parents. In a matter of minutes both boys were sitting wide-eyed wondering what Mr. Walters was going to say.

Mr. Walters said, "I want to thank the boys for their bravery and for caring about someone in trouble. I'm eternally grateful and thankful to have people in my life I can trust. I'd like to offer both you boys a part time job, at a dollar an hour. The job would only take a few hours a week and wouldn't interfere with school. I'll expect you to clean my yard once a week. If you do a good job when you're a little older you can both work in my hardware store."

Wide-eyed, Frankie said, "I'd love to have a job."

Sam replied, "Ditto, I've been looking for a way to make some money."

Their parents sat looking bewildered at the good fortune befalling their families. A dollar an hour was top wages.

Mr. Walters reached in his pocket and handed each boy a bankbook. It had their names written on the front page along with their parent's name. When they opened the bankbook, they seen he had deposited $500.00 in each of the accounts. This was too much. They never dreamed their good deed was going to make them rich.

Mr. Walters said, "Boys, this is your money to do whatever you choose. I think it would be a wise to save it toward an education. If you both save half of what you earn. By the time your ready to go to college, you will have enough money saved to attend the school of your choice. Most children quit school to help the family budget. It is my pleasure to offer both of you the opportunity to continue your education. What you boys did for me was no small thing and your bravery deserves to be rewarded.

"We haven't any children. It makes us happy to do something to help you boys have a good start in life. Using the money the way I'm suggesting isn't mandatory. I put your parents name on the bankbook too. You'll have to consult with them before any withdrawals are made."

For the second time in their life, Frankie and Sam were speechless.

Their parents thanked Mr. and Mrs. Walters for their kindness.

Mrs. Walters said, "I have no idea what I would have done if anything had happened to my husband. The reward is little enough to thank the quick thinking of you brave children for saving his life. I'll look forward to seeing you boys Saturday morning.

Frankie and Sam's parents didn't know what to think of all the good fortune that transpired. A college education would have been unthinkable. Now both Sam and Frankie were going to have an opportunity to choose whatever profession their hearts desired.

Frankie was excited, but he felt a little sad because his brothers and sisters were not included in his stroke of good luck. He wanted to share his good fortune with them. He decided that when he went to work on Saturday, he'd ask Mr. Walters if he'd give both his brothers and his sister a part time job.

Sure enough, Mr. Walters agreed to give the other Stargazer children a part time job too. He hired Joe, Greg, and Angela to work in one of his hardware stores. Lynn was too young to work, so she tagged along with her brother Frankie, and played in the yard while she waited for him to finish cleaning the Walters yard.

Mrs. Walters liked having Lynn visit while her brother worked. She would invite Lynn into the house and allow her to watch TV. Sometimes, Mrs. Walters had the servants prepare tea parties on the veranda and she'd sit patiently listening to Lynn prattle on for hours.

The Walters had a private swimming pool, along with a tennis and basketball court. They invited Frankie and Sam's family to come over to swim or play tennis. They were always sending goodies home with the children. The Walters became very close friends with the entire Stargazer family.

Things were looking up for the Stargazer's. With the children working part time, they were able to save a little money. Nevertheless, Mom still made do and economized as much as she possibly could.

A few more years went by and Joe and Greg both graduated from high school. Angela was a junior and Lynn was going to be thirteen in a few days. All Lynn could think about was that she was going to have her very own birthday party. She was so excited; she could hardly wait for the days to pass.

Lynn couldn't understand why her family was being so quiet about her birthday party. Mom and Dad could see that the closer it got to Lynn's thirteenth birthday, the more apprehensive she became. She kept asking why no one was talking about the theme of the party or what kind of costumes everyone would wear, or why they weren't preparing different kinds of food to serve? They merely told Lynn to have patience.

Lynn's big day finally arrived. She sulked and moped and went to school feeling downhearted. When the school day was over she found Frankie waiting by her classroom door ready to walk home with her. He told her he had to stop by Mr. Walters house and work for an hour and would she mind waiting for him? Feeling sorry for herself she said, "I might as well go with you, no one seems to care that today is my thirteenth birthday. No one planned a party for me."

They arrived at the Walters mansion and walked through the big gates attached to a six-foot high brick fence around the acreage. Lynn had no idea everyone was hiding behind the fence. The minute they stepped inside the gate, family, friends, and the Walters yelled, "Surprise!" She stood there flabbergasted. She could hardly believe her eyes. The back yard was decorated with Chinese Lanterns and a hired band started to play the Happy Birthday song. Several servants were loading the tables with every kind of food imaginable.

There was a table filled with gifts wrapped in pretty paper. It was all so grand and luxurious. She perked up instantly, exclaiming that it was the most beautiful sight she ever saw.

Mom and Dad said they had a hard time keeping the party a secret and they almost spilled the beans. They felt bad knowing she was so miserable the last few days. It turned out that soon after Mrs. Walters heard about the parties the other children had when they turned thirteen; she called Mrs. Stargazer and asked if she could plan Lynn's celebration.

Throughout the party, Lynn remained astounded at the scrumptious food; pretty decorations and the hoopla that was actually taking place on her birthday.

Frankie winked and grinned from ear to ear as he told Lynn, "This is your special day because you're a special gal."

Joe, Greg and Frankie all danced with her. She was especially flattered when Sam asked her to dance. Before tonight all he ever did was tell her to get lost and tease her unmercifully.

Lynn told everyone that she felt like a princess. It was the most wonderful night of her life. The party lasted till eleven o'clock. Everyone thanked the Walters and started to head for home. There were so many people laughing, talking and leaving at the same time, no one, except Frankie noticed the stranger driving back and forth in front of the Walters residence.

When the Stargazers walked in the front door of their house, Frankie was the first to head upstairs. It was such a beautiful starlit night he decided to crawl out the window and sleep on the roof. The moment he laid his head down to stare at the extraordinary star, a picture flashed in the sky of the Walters struggling with someone.

Frankie jumped off the roof and yo, the wings appeared instantly. He flew to the Walters residence. As he approached the residence he spotted a thief holding a gun in Mr. Walters back. He was trying to force him into a car that was parked a few yards down the street. The man was big and kind of stocky. He didn't look like the average criminal. Except for the ski mask he was wearing, he was well dressed.

As Frankie flew straight into the thief his hands turned into the power of a sledgehammer and the force from the blow immediately tumbled the man to the ground.

With one look from Frankie's starlit blue eyes, the thief's hands and legs were securely tied. He picked up the gun and asked the stunned Mr. Walters to run back to the house and call the police. It all happened so fast Mr. Walters didn't see how Frankie accomplished the daring feats while apprehending the thief.

Mr. Walters was being kidnapped for ransom money. The thief tied Mrs. Walters up and locked her in a closet.

Frankie said, "Mr. Walters, go call the police."

Mr. Walters rushed back into his house, freed his wife and called the police. Then the Walter's went outside and helped their chauffer to his feet. Frankie was standing by the criminal, still lying on the ground, out cold and bound to the hilt.

Within minutes the police came and took the kidnapper away. They couldn't understand how a boy like Frankie could apprehend the thief so quickly and thoroughly. Or how he happened to be in the area, at the very precise time Mr. Walters needed help.

Frankie was fifteen years old, but he was already six feet tall and very muscular. Even as a small child, he was never considered to be a wimp. He always seemed to hold his own and never took anything from tough hoodlums that tried to bully the kids in his neighborhood.

After the police left the scene of the crime, Mr. and Mrs. Walters, the bodyguard, Don, and Frankie all went into the house. Mrs. Walters fixed a pot of coffee and tended to Don's wounds.

"What happened after everyone left the party?" Frankie asked

The Walters explained that shortly after everyone left the party, the thief attached a rope ladder on the gate and climbed over.

Their chauffer heard the dogs barking and came running out of the guesthouse, where he lived. The burglar hid in the bushes, jumped out and hit him in the head with the butt of a gun. Then, he shot the locks off the door, went up to the Walters bedroom, tied up Mrs. Walters and put her in the closet. The kidnapper told Mr. Walters if he didn't come quietly, he would shoot his wife. Before they knew what had occurred, the thief was walking toward the car with Mr. Walters.

Mr. Walters said, "That's when you showed up Frankie. You know the rest of the story. But how you surmised something was wrong is kind of vague?"

Frankie said, "I saw the stranger drive by as we were leaving the party. It was late. Not many people are on the streets at that time of night. As I was walking home, I wondered what the stranger was up to."

Frankie knew better than to tell anyone that he seen a vision of the scene that was taking place at the Walter's residence.

Mr. Walters said, "Frankie, once again, you've saved my life. I don't know how to thank you. I'm beginning to wonder if you're my guardian angel. How can I ever repay you?"

Frankie said, "Please sir, I assure you, I'm no angel. You have done so much for my family already. I don't want you to give me another thing. You're not just my boss; you have been my friend too. I'd rather not have anything more said about the incident."

The Walters insisted that Don drive Frankie home.

On the way home, Don said, "Frankie, The Walters are such kind people. They are wealthy, but they don't flaunt it. They're the first people to lend a helping hand to those in need. I'm afraid of what might have happened to the Walters, if you hadn't come along when you did."

Frankie said, "It's over with. Don't be hard on your self. There's my house, Thanks for the ride."

Mom and Dad were sitting in the front room, waiting for him to walk through the front door. The minute Frankie walked in they told him that they heard a noise and went to check it out when they noticed he was gone. They had no idea why he would leave the house so late. They were about to call the police and report him missing.

Frankie didn't say anything, nor did he tell them what transpired at the Walters residence. Not aware of the events that took place, his parents lectured him about leaving the house in the dead of night. They told him he was grounded and couldn't go anywhere for a week. They ended the discussion and went back to bed.

During the course of the same evening, Sam couldn't sleep so he sat on the window seat, staring into space. When he saw the lights on in the Stargazer's house he decided to go over to see what was happening. He ended up spending the night at Frankie's house. But not before leaving a note telling his parents where he was.

Sam and Frankie went out on the roof, so they could be alone. Laughing and cutting up, they talked way into the early morning hours. Suddenly Sam stopped laughing and got very serious. He said, "Frankie, we've known each other all these years. I know when something's going on with you. Want to talk about it?"

"Not really," Frankie remarked. He ended up telling Sam about the burglar saga, at the Walters house after the party.

Sam said, "I think there's more to the story than you're telling me."

Frankie replied, "The only thing that happened, is that I was the only one to see the stranger drive by Mr. Walters home when the party was over. I decided to walk by and see if the unfamiliar person was still lurking around. I'm awfully tired now. Maybe, I'll tell you the whole story someday but not right now."

Sam said, "Oky Doky friend, I won't pressure you for more details tonight. You can tell me more when you're ready. Let's go to sleep. I'm beat too."

The next day the boys slept late. When they finally went down to join the family for breakfast, Frankie's parents confronted him with the town newspaper. Lo and behold, on the front page of the paper was the story of the Walters unfortunate saga. Frankie was dubbed a hero despite his unassuming nature to keep it quiet. The police gave the story to the local newspaper.

Frankie was overwhelmed when he read the paper. He didn't want anyone to make a fuss. He especially didn't want anyone to ask him any questions.

His parents were surprised to see their sons name splashed across the headlines after he acted so nonchalant about leaving the house last night. The amazing story about Frankie's whereabouts appearing in the paper was a little too much to take in.

Mom said, "Frankie, I don't understand why you didn't tell us about this last night. Do you know you could have been hurt? Worse than that, you could have been killed. The paper said the burglar had a gun."

Frankie replied, "Please, Mom and Dad it was nothing. I just acted out of fear for the Walters. It is no big thing. I didn't do anything anyone else wouldn't have done if they had seen someone in trouble."

It wasn't the end of the incident, but for now, the family stopped bugging him.

Grandma and Grandpa came over for breakfast, as they had done every Saturday morning for as long as Frankie could remember and they said plenty. By and large, they were worried he was tempting fate rescuing people by himself.

Grandpa said, "Frankie, you should have called the police when you noticed the stranger driving in the area.

Frankie remarked, " You can't call the police about every stranger that drives through the town of Blue Rivers."

All through breakfast, Frankie noticed Joe was staring intently at him. After Sam went home, Frankie walked up the stairs and went directly into his room. A few minutes later Joe got up from the table and went to Frankie's room too.

Joe ambled into Frankie's bedroom and sat in the armchair by the window. He said, "Okay Frankie, what gives? Do you want to tell me what's going on?"

"I don't know what you're talking about. Nothings going on," Frankie said.

Joe's said," I doubt that. I've been watching you all morning. I could see you were hiding something behind your baby blues. All I'm saying for now is don't hesitate to let me be there for you if you need me. Besides, I've seen and heard about some of the out of the ordinary spectacles going on with you."

Frankie innocently asked, "What exactly do you mean?"

Joe said, "I have to go to work now. I'll meet you on the roof tonight at bedtime and we can talk about it then."

CHAPTER 5…
FRANKIE'S ACTIONS

Frankie thought, "Oh me o my, what do I do now? Everyone wants to shake my hand. They're calling me a hero. I'm going to crawl under my bed. I'm never coming out again. Why did the police have to call the newspaper and make a big deal out of everything?"

That evening when Joe came home from work he found that Frankie had been hiding in his room the entire day. The first thing Frankie told Joe was, "I'm not ever going to leave this room again. I can't take people making a fuss over me. Even my girlfriend Cynthia is calling me a hero."

Joe said, "My dear brother, Frankie, even I have to admit what you did was quite spectacular for a fifteen-year-old. Are you ready to tell me about it? I don't mean the story your telling everyone else, but the real story. You see, I know more than you think I do. Greg and I are both wise to a few events, involving your feats of heroism.

"We kept quiet because we knew you didn't want anyone to make a big thing out of your behavior. For instance, I saw you climb a dangerously tall dead tree to rescue a kitten that was afraid to come back down. More than that, we knew about the time you rescued Margie from a gang of thugs, about to harm her. She told me they cornered her on her way home from work, dragged her into a dark alley and threw her to the ground. All of a sudden, you appeared out of nowhere. You knocked the four bullies out cold, and then you escorted her home.

"Widow Morton, from the candy store downtown, confided that two men were trying to rob her store one day. Again, you appeared out of nowhere, hog tied the thieves with a rope and told her to call the police. You begged her not to reveal the way you rescued her. She told the police she didn't know the name of her rescuer.

"Not to mention the time Judy got off the school bus and a car followed her up the drive. One of the men jumped out, grabbed her and threw her in their car.

"You appeared out of nowhere, stood in front of the speeding car, only to have it hit you. The car crumpled up like an accordion, but not before the men aimed and shot a gun directly in your face. The bullets whizzed every which way and never came close to hitting you.

"Judy said, you pulled her safely out of the car and stayed to comfort her until help arrived. She didn't have a scratch on her. The criminals were scrunched up in the car, unable to move an inch. You left a second before the police arrived.

"You're bribing all of the people you rescue into letting you remain anonymous. They're so grateful they respected your wishes. They wanted someone in you're family to know what you did for them, and how thankful they felt toward my brother. Every one you helped said they simply couldn't get over the way you put your life on the line for their welfare.

"What gives Frankie? Greg and I are certain something big is going on. How long do you think you can manage to keep the incidents you're involved in secret from the family or for that matter, from the police and the rest of the town? Certainly you're aware of the fact that you're getting quite a reputation among the law enforcement of this community. The people you rescued respected your wishes, and didn't tell anyone other than Greg and I. No matter how hard you try to keep your deeds a secret, stories are filtering out."

Frankie replied, "I don't know what to say. I hesitate to tell anyone. I don't want everyone making a fuss over me. Besides, my family doesn't seem to accept my stories. Okay, I'll let you in on a few of my secrets, but if I see you look at me with disbelief and doubt in your eyes, I can't continue to explain. All of it is miraculously astounding, astonishing, and amazing even to me. I can't imagine what you'll think when I'm through telling you."

"All right, try me," Joe remarked.

Frankie said, "Well Joe, it all started when I had my accident and I was in a coma, I thought I was merely living through one of the most unbelievable fantastic dreams of all time. At first, I thought it was nothing more than that. You know, just a delusional reverie, but it was really happening. As you know I tried to tell my family but everyone hushed me up and thought I was fabricating fairytales.

"I don't need to tell you the way Mom and Dad kept taking me to the doctor and staring at me with a sad pitiful look on their face. I couldn't stand to see them look so forlorn each time I tried to say something about my dream.

"I don't fault anyone for not believing me. I couldn't believe it either, until one night when I was sleeping on the roof, I had the most fabulous adventure anyone could ever have and maybe ever will. I don't know about that though because if it could happen to me, maybe it did happen to others and no one ever knew about it, What would you say if I told you I can fly and breathe no matter how high into space I go, or what planet I land on?"

Joe replied, "How could you expect me to even consider something as improbable as that bit of malarkey? There has to be an explanation."

Frankie said, "There, you see. You're looking for a logical explanation when there isn't any. You're not going to accept anything I say, so how can I confide more, and there's plenty more where that came from that you're not going to fathom."

Joe remarked, "It's not that I don't want to believe you. I want to trust that all your telling me is the truth. I simply can't comprehend it as being real. It all sounds incredibly, implausible and mind-boggling."

Frankie went on to say, "Okay Joe, before I tell you any more, lets wake Greg up. Then, lets go out on the roof. It will be easier to show you both at the same time rather then try to explain any further."

Being careful not to wake the rest of the family, Joe woke Greg up and they quietly followed Frankie out the window. The moment the boys stepped out on the roof, Frankie's wings zapped out and scooped Joe and Greg up on his back. Before either one could close their mouth that flew wide open, they were airborne. The three boys were bounding off into space, passing by asteroids, planets, and stars.

Joe and Greg's eyes were as big as saucers as they hung on for dear life. They didn't know that even if he flew upside down, there was no way they would have fallen off his back, for no harm could befall them as long as they were with Frankie.

Before they could say, 'Bo Jangles,' Frankie soared to a planet he had visited once before when testing some of his abilities.

When their feet were on solid ground, both boys walked a little wobbly and were shaking their heads in disbelief at the events that happened the second they set foot on the roof. It was more than incredible that Joe and Greg were totally unafraid. They were astonished their brother Frankie had the awesome power to fly and astounded at their own adventurous flight. The sights they we're beholding on another planet with their very own eyes were breathtaking.

The planet Frankie landed on was as alluring as the earth, with green thick grass rolling across the sweetest smelling meadows, spattered with the most stunning flowers as far as the eye could see. There were honeysuckle trees glowing with budding flowers the same radiant colors of a rainbow directly after the sun first peeks intensely through bursting rain clouds. The planets sky was gorgeously wafted with different, striking shades of blues.

The three Stargazer boys walked across the meadow talking a mile a minute about the way the fascinating colors reminded them of a rainbow. They reminisced about the way they loved running outdoors to see if they could find a rainbow after a rainstorm. They loved to watch the brilliant colors fade into beautiful pastel shades as the rainbow faded.

Sometimes, they'd spot a double rainbow adorning the sky with colors reaching right down to the earth. Of course, when they were younger they wondered if they could find the fabled pot of gold that was supposed to be sitting at the end of the rainbow. Totally fascinated with the picturesque view, Greg shared a Bible lesson he learned in Sunday school about the way God put the colored bow in the sky as a covenant between God and man to symbolize his promise, never to allow the entire world to be destroyed by a flood ever again.

Soon the three boys arrived at an outstanding two-story house constructed with colored bricks and decorated with white hand carved designs in the rounded wooden window frames. It had a porch around the entire house. There were enormous trees shading the yard with beautiful flowers that were sprinkled in colorful splendor everywhere.

Frankie seemed to be acquainted with the three very magnificent looking people that came out of the house to greet him as if he were an old friend. They said, "Frankie what a nice surprise. We're glad you came to visit us again."

Frankie said, "It's nice to see you all again too. These are my brothers, Joe and Greg Stargazer. Then turning to his brothers, Frankie said, "I want you both to meet Matthew and Matilda Stoerr and their daughter Melinda."

Greg and Joe stood speechless for what seemed like an eternity.

When they got their bearings back they said, "Holy cow! This is unbelievable. Where in God's creation are we?"

Don't be frightened, Matthew said. "You're on a peaceful planet called, 'Moonazer.' It is similar to the planet earth but unlike your planet, we live in tranquility and harmony. There is no crime here."

Amazed and at the same time, Joe and Greg both said, "No crime!"

Matthew repeated his words, "No, there is absolutely no crime. There is a force around our planet that prevents anyone with evil intent in his or her heart from landing on planet Moonazer. If they come anywhere near Moonazer, they are tossed into the depths of the dreaded, Black planet that is called 'Nomed.' It was created especially for all who endorse black spirits and harbor and delight in wickedness."

Joe asked, "How could that be? How can the very air know what's in someone's heart?"

Matthew explained, "It is not the air that prevents them from landing. It is the hedge of protection around the planet that keeps Moonazer safe. Our founding Father put it there from the beginning of time. Frankie was able to come through the shield of protection and land safely because he has no evil in his heart. Joe and Greg, you need to understand that your brother would never have been allowed to bring you here and land safely on our planet if either one of you embraced evil in your heart. Since your motives are not evil but good, you were able to visit Moonazer in peace. Now come inside the house and have something to eat, and then I'll show you around the farmstead before you journey back to earth."

Joe and Greg kept pinching themselves to see if it they were sleeping or awake, if this was real or unreal. The boys thought their adventure into space and landing on Moonazer would have to be classified as tremendously overwhelming. It was putting it mildly to say, that they were merely enthralled.

After they realized it was real, Joe and Greg had to stop pinching themselves. For the more they saw and heard, the harder they pinched. They started feeling unbearable pain from squeezing their arm. Tiny red welts were beginning to appear on their skin.

They all walked into the stunning home that was simply, but beautifully decorated. The walls of the rooms were colored in every different shade of blue imaginable. The furniture was hand carved in a Victorian style. The long ornate table was already set for the three boys and food was waiting to be served. It was as if they knew the boys were coming to visit. It was inconceivably mind blowing to be sitting and eating with other humans living on another planet in the Universe, God only knows where. It was weird to see the china dishes and silverware pattern were exactly the same as the ones

Grandma and Grandpa used every Sunday when they all gathered around the table for lunch after attending church.

Most of the food the women prepared looked a lot like some of the food Mom cooked and served to company. However, there were a few things they never seen or tasted before. The table was festooned with caramelized strawberries dipped in chocolate. There was an array of decorated kinds of candy and cakes imaginable. There were even flavors they couldn't imagine. Some of the fruit was odd shaped and the same blue, orange, red, purple, green, and yellow shades of color as the budding flowers in the magnolia trees. Everything tasted scrumptious.

All through the meal Greg and Melinda couldn't keep their eyes off one another. After the meal was over Matilda and Melinda started clearing the table and doing the kitchen chores.

Matthew said, "Come on boys. While the women are cleaning up, I want to show you the pond in our back yard."

They walked around the yard viewing the clean white picket fence painted with a tiny pink rose design. The back yard was fabulously landscaped with the same kind of trees and flowers like the ones they viewed in the fields. The leaves in the trees touched one another in a way that actually resembled an umbrella. It looked as though nothing could float through the covering the leaves made high in the air around the entire yard.

Observing the birds singing and flying to and fro, the boys noticed the way they resembled tropical birds. There were peacocks and huge parrots. The birds seemed tame. They came right up to the boys, and either sat on their shoulders or walked right beside them. They reached the pond and gasped at the beauty of the fish swimming close to the surface of the water. Some of the fish had the same spots, stripes, designs and colors as the bird's overhead.

Joe was eager and energized as he said, "The fish and the birds remind me of a school trip our entire class went on during our freshman year in high school. We went to a museum and observed every kind of bird imaginable. There were aquatic fish tanks in the museum too. The tanks were filled with fish patterned with the same colors as the birds. I couldn't help but think, how remarkable it is that God has the ability to create fish in the deep waters to look exactly like the birds of the air. I simply can't grasp being on another planet far from earth, privileged to see the same spectacle again.

"There is just no way something of this magnitude could be created by anyone but the awesome artistry of a higher being. How could anyone believe man evolved from a monkey or an ape? It is beyond my knowledge that the theory of evolution could ever come into being. I think it takes more for someone not to believe in a Creator than it takes to believe there is a God. Only the Almighty, Holy God could have created and accomplished the mighty works that brought the Universe, along with else everything into being, in the harmony with which it all works together."

The boys wondered who the founding father of the planet was that Matthew spoke of, but they hesitated to ask that question.

Matthew said, "Joe and Greg, I should tell you that your brother Frankie knew that both of you boys were going to be two of his allies in the scheme of things to come or he couldn't have brought you here. The first time Frankie arrived on our planet, we knew he was coming and that he was going to be a force fighter and obey the voice of the mighty 'IAM.'

"Sit down, boys, and let's talk a while before you go back to planet earth. I've been appointed to explain some of the marvels you've witnessed. I need your undivided attention to accept what I'm about to tell you. I can't answer all the inquisitiveness I see in your eyes.

"So far, you've witnessed sights and experienced things no one will ever accept. It's crucial to acknowledge, that it is no accident that you were brought to my home tonight. Your brother has been chosen to fight crime and evil. He has already started the destiny he is about to fulfill. I'm sure it must be very hard to believe and understand why or how he came to be filled with abilities that are unimaginable to the naked eye. Nevertheless, you perceived some of them in action.

"Frankie is able to see into the spirit world. He's aware of wicked forces that cause fear to all mankind. His powers of force will be used to fight whatever obstacles and conflicts come his way.

"You've both been chosen to be his cohorts, and his friend, as well as his brothers. He needs you both to support him in every way, and lend a hand from time to time. Assist him in covering his tracks, to remain as anonymous as he possibly can. For the conflicts will become greater and greater. Most of what he has been appointed to accomplish won't make sense to anyone. Believe and trust your brother. By having confidence in him, you're placing trust in a far greater power than your brother.

"Most importantly, keep in mind, that you're not allowed to expose anything concerning your adventures thus far. Frankie has the capability to take away memory of all that took place tonight. He has asked that his two brothers be able to retain the information they have been privy to on this day. There may come a time that the voice of IAM will permit both of you to see more of the awesome force Frankie has within his being. Perhaps sometime in the near future, IAM might even allow you to go on a secret mission you're brother Frankie will be assigned to complete.

"Here comes Matilda and Melinda so let's say no more. Anyway, It's just about time for your flight home. It has been an honor to make your acquaintance. We shall meet again."

It was too much to take in and once again, Joe and Greg were without words.

They thanked Matthew, Matilda, and Melinda for their kind hospitality. Zap! In a split second the three boys were crawling back in the upstairs window of their own, home sweet home. Exhausted, they hopped into bed and were sound asleep the moment their heads hit the pillow.

The next morning, Joe and Greg couldn't stop smiling at one another. It was exhilarating to think they shared such an enormous secret. They had a lot of unanswered questions swirling in their head. For the time being they were too happy to think about them. The adventure they shared last evening was fresh in their brains. All they could say to each other was, "Wow! It's so cool to have a brother that's a force fighter, a real live hero."

Joe and Greg walked to work in a daze. Frankie took off to pick up Sam for school. All was back to normal. Whoops, did someone say normal? Nothing will ever be normal again.

CHAPTER 6… APPEARANCE OF A WICKED BEING

On the way to school Sam said, "Frankie where were you last night? I snuck over to your house, climbed up the tree, crawled on the roof, and then I climbed in the window. I went into the bedroom and neither you, nor Joe, or Greg was there so I went back home. I know your parents didn't know you guys were out messing around. I called on the telephone once but they said you were sleeping."

Being close to the Stargazer boys, there were times Sam went with them when they slipped out at night. The boys would sneak out the upstairs window and slide down the drainpipe, leading from the roof to the ground. They weren't really getting into any real mischief. They merely fooled around the neighborhood or walked to the local restaurant, simply to have a coke and shoot the bull. Afterwards, they snuck back in the house and slipped into bed while no one was the wiser, or so they thought. There were times the boys parents woke up and checked on them. Needless to say, they were punished for sneaking out late at night.

Mom would say, "Joe, you're the oldest child. I expect you to know better. You're supposed to be an example for your younger brothers."

Frankie told Sam, "It's a long story. I don't feel like talking about it right now."

"Why are you being so mysterious?" Sam asked. "I thought we we're best friends and we we're going to share all our secrets."

Frankie sighed as he remarked, "Quit bugging me to tell you at this very moment. This is colossal stuff, it's not like I can say, pinky swear. When I'm ready to tell you, I have to be absolutely certain that it won't go any further. My story, could blow the lid of knowledge sky high."

Sam said, "I've heard that same old adage for a long time now. When is the time going to be right? I'm beginning to feel like you don't trust me."

"It's not a matter of trust, it's bigger than that," Frankie replied. "I'll think about it and let you know one way or the other on Saturday night."

Sam retorted, "All right my friend. I'll stop prodding you for now."

Frankie wasn't quite sure what to tell him. He knew he had to be careful, who he shared his secrets with. But this was Sam. The one person he shared everything with. Frankie didn't know how much longer he could get by hiding his destiny from his best friend. More than that, Sam was more like a brother.

That evening before Frankie fell asleep he whispered, IAM, what should I do? I'm not sure if Sam is supposed to know. I can't keep up the façade much longer. He's always around. I keep making excuses for the times I disappear and he can't find me. If I'm not hanging out with Sam, my parents become suspicious and question my whereabouts."

Sometime during the night after Frankie finally fell asleep, he dreamed the voice of IAM was telling him that it was all right to take Sam into his confidence. His friend would not reveal his secret for eventually Sam will be a part of the same team you're serving on. In due time a few more people will see your force in action. They will stand by your side to assist and support your actions.

When Frankie woke up the next morning he felt refreshed. He knew without a doubt that he heard the voice of IAM while he was sleeping. He was relieved that he could finally share his secret with his best friend.

Saturday evening after Sam and Frankie were through working, they went to grab a bite to eat. Then, they decided to take in a movie. On the way home, a homeless drifter that was roaming the streets stopped the boys. They noticed the man was especially tall, unshaven and grubby looking. He told them he hadn't eaten in several days and he was hungry. The man asked if they had a few dollars they could give him so he could buy something to eat.

The boys were taught not to trust strangers, but they felt sorry for the beggar so they dug deep in their pockets. Between the two of them, they had around a dollar and fifty cents. They handed the money to the man and started down the street. After Sam and Frankie had walked a few blocks they noticed the drifter was still following them. They decided to turn around and walk straight toward him, to ask him why he was following them. Surely the man knew they gave him their last dime. When Sam and Frankie caught up to the beggar, they said, "Get lost. We don't have any more money."

It took the boys by surprise when the man quickly grabbed Sam, pulled out a gun and told Frankie to beat it or he'd shoot his friend. Then, unexpectedly the beggar pointed the gun at Frankie and shot him square in the face.

Strangely enough, the instant the man pulled the trigger, Frankie glimpsed another figure standing next to the drifter, egging him on to shoot again. The bullet didn't so much as scratch Frankie. Before the bum could fire another shot, Frankie's fist changed into a hammer, shot forward and knocked the gun out of the beggar's hand. With one look from his sapphire, blue eyes, the man was thrown next to a tree and was firmly tied from head to foot with thick silver wire. The man was out cold and bound from head to foot. The perpetrator was unable to utter a word.

Stunned and shook up by the drifter's actions to harm them, Sam's words were slurred as he asked Frankie, "What the devil just happened?"

Frankie said, "Quick, let's run to my house and call the police to pick this maniac up."

The vagrant, looking terribly dumbfounded, started to moan. He was tied so firmly, he couldn't move a muscle.

On the way to Frankie's house, Sam still wasn't able to talk clearly, so he whispered, "it's astounding! The man shot you,

Frankie, and you didn't get a scratch, how can this be?"

Frankie said, "Stop worrying Sam. Everything's going to be okay. Please, don't say a word to my parent's about all the things that happened. Let's call the police first and then we'll tell them, we encountered a bum that tried to hustle us. I'll explain the rest to you later."

They stopped talking and ran the rest of the way home. They called the police and gave the location of the assailant.

The police found the bum, just the way the boys said they would. The gun was still lying on the ground near the tree he was tied to. Later on, the police ran a background check on the man. He turned out to be an escaped felon.

In the meantime, the boy's put their heads together to figure out what they were going to tell people.

Frankie said, "We have to omit parts of the story. You can't tell anyone the bum shot me or that you seen the unbelievable way I apprehended the perpetrator in a manner you've never seen before.

"Remember what I told you Sam. You mustn't let my parents know the entire story because they wouldn't be able to deal with it. They would probably haul me off somewhere to be examined until they had an answer they could live with. The problem is, I couldn't live with them keeping me under close scrutiny. Trust me Sam. I'll tell you the details and the reason I didn't get hurt when we're alone in my room. I know you're more than curious to know the reason why the bullet didn't harm me and why I was able to handle apprehending him in a way out manner."

The once small town of 'Blue Rivers' had its share of crime, but an incident of this magnitude was unheard of. It was bad enough when the thief held the Walters hostage for money, but this man actually shot Frankie and he was going to do bodily harm to Sam, too. Crime was on the rise and it wasn't as safe in the streets as it had been merely two years ago.

Even though this was a stranger passing through. It was probably just a fluke that he happened to stop in their town. The boys thought about all the times they snuck out of their house to roam around, feeling safe no matter where they went.

Mom and Dad didn't know what to think when Frankie & Sam rushed in the house grabbed the phone and called the police. They were both disheveled and out of breath. Mom examined the boys and par to course, she wanted to take them to the hospital. Sam and Frankie said they were a little shaken up, but they were tough and were both okay. After hugging and kissing them, Mom fixed them up with her home remedy of cookies and milk. She waited outside the bathroom door until both boys took a bath and put their pajamas on, and then she tucked them into bed. It didn't matter that Frankie and Sam were almost sixteen, she still treated them as if they were five years old. Although Sam and Frankie wouldn't admit it out loud, age didn't seem to be a barrier tonight; they loved Mom's steadfast love comforting them after the harrowing experience they endured.

Satisfied that the boys were okay, Mom and Dad finally went to their room to go to bed. The boys waited until they were certain both parents were asleep before they got out from under the covers and sat on Frankie's bed. They put a blanket over their heads in a tent fashion and talked way into the night.

Frankie confessed the entire story to Sam. Starting with the first day and the strange things he encountered in his vision on the rainbow colored star. He told Sam the voice of his friend IAM was the source of his power, the one that protects him, and the sole reason the bullets from the gun couldn't hurt him.

Although Sam was overwhelmed at the story he was hearing, oddly enough, he believed everything Frankie told him without question. Sam made him repeat the story about planet 'Moonazer' five times. He wouldn't go to sleep, until Frankie promised to take him there.

Frankie thought it was best to omit telling his friend about the handsome white figure he seen standing beside the bum, for he was certain Sam didn't see it. He couldn't forget the way the figure had his hand on the gun at the same time the vagrant pulled the trigger.

Sam said, "Frankie, you never have to worry about me. I will never reveal or betray all that you've confided about your powerful fate of force. I've seen the tiny white stars in your eyes from time to time. I used to think it was from the glow of the light hitting you a certain way. Your eyes sparkle so much when you're excited, I simply thought of it as part of your makeup. I'll never, not in a million years, ever tell anyone your secrets, even under the threat of torture. We will always be best friends and as close to one another as I feel toward you tonight. You saved my life, Frankie Stargazer. My friend, I will be eternally grateful to you for the rest of my life."

After talking for hours, both boys finally nodded off into a deep sleep.

In the morning, Sam went to church with Frankie's family and then went to Grandpa and Grandma Stargazer's house for lunch.

After lunch, Frankie and Sam were exhausted. They both fell asleep on the sofa. The dog curled up between the boys and took a nap with them. Mom and Dad were relaxing in the easy chairs. The rest of the children were spending the afternoon at their friend's house.

It was such a relaxing, peaceful Sunday afternoon. No one dwelled on the danger the boys faced the night before. The Stargazers were thankful everyone was okay and they were all together, safe and sound.

Monday morning came all to soon. Frankie was taking a shower, when out of the blue, the figure he saw standing next to the predator, popped into his head. The figure was extremely handsome, with long blonde hair flowing to his shoulders. His clothes were glowing white. They were made like a one-piece suit, with a glimmering gold sash around the waist. He thought of the way the figure had his hand on top of the beggar's hand, as if he were pulling the trigger too.

He could see it all so clear. Where in blazes did that man come from? He just popped up out of nowhere the instant the man was about to commit the horrendous crime of murder. The strange figure was smiling all the while he was in the act of helping the vagrant destroy an innocent life.

Frankie knew if it wasn't for IAM and his predestined force, he would have been frightened out of his wits. He'd probably be sitting in the corner of an institution somewhere, flipping his lip with the tip of his finger.

The police wondered how two young boys could apprehend the convicted felon so securely and the kind of wire that was used to hold the escaped convict. They had it examined by experts, but it wasn't like anything they'd ever seen. The metal was shiny and unbreakable. Frankie couldn't disclose where the wire came from or how he managed to tie the man to the tree.

Then, the police assumed the only way Frankie could have tied up the vagrant with the shiny metal was that the wire must have been lying on the ground near the tree. It was a mystery that they set aside for the time being but they continued to speculate on the incident.

CHAPTER 7…
THE UNKNOWN

Frankie's seventeenth birthday was fast approaching. He didn't want his family to plan a party this year. Financially, the Stargazer's were doing pretty well now. They invested in one of the newer TV models on the market. Their assets had grown considerably since Joe and Greg graduated high school and were working full time.

Angela had grown into a gracious, gorgeous young lady about to graduate high school. She was planning to marry Richard Phillips soon after graduation. He was a few years older than her and he was about to graduate from Junior College. Technology was increasing and the economy was booming. Jobs were plentiful and wages were climbing to a new all time high.

Lynn was fifteen now and turning into a real beauty. Frankie began to notice Sam stopped teasing her whenever he came over. Sam tried to hide the fact that he was becoming very fond of Lynn.

Sam started to watch over Lynn whenever the guys started to act like they wanted to take her out on a date. He always checked them out and hung around the house until Lynn came home. Later on, Sam would ask her to do something with him so she wouldn't have time to accept invitations from other boys. It was sort of funny when we caught on to what Sam was up to and how much he liked Lynn. We teased Sam unmercifully and he'd turn beet red and deny it, claiming Lynn was like his little sister. He didn't want some redneck taking advantage of her.

In the meantime, Sam basked in the newfound knowledge that his best friend shared with him. Frankie felt so much better that he could pull Joe, Greg and Sam into his confidence and share his powerful, adventurous, undisclosed secrets.

Frankie regretted that his parents still didn't know of his power and the things he was becoming involved in. Understanding only to well, how they would have reacted, he wanted to protect them too.

On the other hand, Frankie thought it was strange there were times Grandma and Grandpa acted like they knew what Frankie was up too, but they never did let on. They loved having their grandchildren be bop in and out of their house to spend the night. The grandparents always let the children know what a comfort and a joy they were.

They enjoyed fussing over the grandchildren. They we're always making homemade gifts to shower them with each time they walked in the door. Sometimes it was easier to confide in Grandma and Grandpa if something was troubling them than it was to tell their parents. Some of the neighborhood children along with Sam felt like they could turn to Grandma and Grandpa as if they were their very own grandparents. It was great having our homes close together.

It took a long while before we figured out one of the lesson's Gramps was trying to teach us when he kept telling us, "If you hoot with the owls by night, you can't soar with the eagles by day."

Grandpa liked kidding and teasing people. We used to think that he was a hoot. He was also an excellent musician and he helped us form our own band.

As the oldest one in the band, along with playing lead guitar, I was in charge of lining up jobs and scheduling practice sessions. Greg played drums, Sam played bass and Frankie played rhythm guitar and was the lead singer. The band was called the "Stargazers and the Stars." We we're pretty good and extremely popular among teen crowds. We played during town celebrations. Not only was it fun to get together and have a jam session, we made a few extra dollars too.

One evening the band put their heads together and decided to see if they could win one of the prizes the town was presenting to the best band, during a battle of the bands contest it was holding. First prize was a brand new motor scooter for each band member. We got together and practiced every night for several weeks.

The night of the contest arrived. The Stargazer boys and Sam put on the matching shirts Mom Stargazer made for the occasion. There were going to be five other bands in the contest. The night of the concert, the road around the area where the bands were going to play was closed to traffic so people could have an old fashioned street dance.

As the evening wore on a gang of rough looking boys from the next town arrived on motorcycles. They started swaggering around and were making pests of themselves. They were consuming alcohol and acting obnoxious. Everyone tried to ignore them the best they could.

It was finally time for 'Stargazer and the Stars' to play. We set up our instruments and started to play the first song. Man, we were really swinging! It was fun playing outdoors in the moonlight. All of a sudden, the hoodlums came near the bandstand. They started jeering and hollering. We were so distracted we stopped playing. The police patrolling the area took over the situation and quieted the gang down. We started playing again. The band started to really rock and roll. The kids were dancing, clapping their hands and having a good old time. It was over all to soon. It was time for the judges to make a final decision.

"We thought we didn't have a chance to win because of the gang's disturbing cat sounds, we started to take the instruments to the car. While we were putting our instruments in the trunk of the car, we heard the announcers booming voice over the loudspeaker announce that the winning band is the, "Stargazer and the Star's.'

"We jumped up and down saying, "Man alive we won. Whoopee! There was screaming, and applause, and people congratulating, and patting us on the back. We stood awe struck that we actually won the contest.

"Our joy was short lived. The festivities turned to chaos directly after the moment of glory. The hoodlums had started a rumble. It happened so fast. No one really knew what actually took place. Seconds after the rumble started.

Frankie was in complete control. "With a flash of his eyes he froze every single person in their tracks. He stacked the hooligan's in a pile, one on top the other. Placing the smallest one on the top of the pile, until they resembled a triangle. He secured them with some sort of material that looked like a huge blanket, until they couldn't move a hair.

"Just as fast as Frankie froze the crowd, he flashed his eyes again and everyone was coherent again. No one had any recall of anything, except that the rumble was over just as quickly as it had started."

The crowd thought the police had put down the riot, so they praised the police for what they believed to be quick confinement of the situation.

Joe knew that whatever happened, had something to do with Frankie. He thought of how awesome Frankie was. It was hard to believe he was his brother, but he was very thankful that he was.

Although Matthew, from planet Moonazer, told us our brother would perform wonders, at the time it was too much to fathom. There are no words to describe all the things that went through my mind when I saw the hoodlums apprehended so quickly. How cool it was no one remembers a thing that took place right before his or her very eyes.

When it was all said and done, even Frankie had a look of astonishment on his face.

Joe asked Frankie, "Why do you look so shocked and apprehensive?

Frankie said, "This was no small issue. There's so much more going on during skirmishes that doesn't meet the eye. It happened during the first few seconds the hoodlums started to rumble. In truth, I'm kind of worried about all it entails. I never thought the battles I'd encounter would involve things that have nothing to do with the stuff our eyes see in the natural realm. I don't exactly know where to begin, so I'll start with the night the escaped convict grabbed Sam. I didn't reveal to a soul that just as the vagrant pulled the trigger on the gun, I caught a glimpse of someone standing right next to him. His hand was on the trigger too.

"At first, I thought I was seeing things. In reality, it was factual. I saw a man wearing a white suit with a gold sash around his waist. He was taunting the fugitive to harm us. He disappeared as fast as he appeared, but not before he glared at me with smoldering eyes. All the while he was enticing the bum to kill me, he had a smile on his face. The pupils in his eyes were pitch black. They kind of resembled python snake eyes. I put it on a back burner thinking I was seeing things that weren't really there, but tonight there he was again.

'This time he had other spirit looking men with him. They were dressed in red suits with gold sashes around their waist. They had the same kind of blazing snake eyes. They were all tempting and taunting the gang to hurt people. I'm very much aware that no one else could see the unnatural spook scene I've been viewing in the midst of a battle.

"Some of the hoodlums had weapons hidden in their jackets and pants pockets. The instant I seen the knives and the guns, I disintegrated them before they could use them. Please Joe, don't say this sounds far fetched. I already know it does. As God is my witness, it's the truth. I was forewarned about fighting crime, but I don't have any idea what kind of spook scene I'm seeing in the background, and that's scary. I need to know who those invisible people are and what are they doing here on earth. How do I handle combating men that appear and disappear? I've got to contact IAM real soon and find out what the heck is happening.

"The ghostly figures are misleading. They appear to be handsome and clean cut. I know without a doubt, they are heinous and evil. I can see them tormenting people, while they are actually using them to harm others."

Joe said, "Frankie, my boy, to tell you the truth, I'm speechless. I don't have the insight or any answers to anything connected to your destiny. I'm here for you to lean on brother, but I'm not sure about any of your powers, or anything, else you're telling me now. I'm not even sure why I was picked to know my younger brother is struggling with things that are way beyond my limited knowledge. It's hard to grasp the fact that your encountering battles and forces for someone or something you have never seen called, IAM.

"I've got to admit, everything you're telling me seems unreal and unbelievable. Nonetheless, I do trust your words to be the unadulterated truth. The fact remains, I'm confused, totally overwhelmed, and dumbfounded at the things you've just told me."

After all that's happened, at this point in time Frankie was also feeling the same emotions Joe felt. He didn't mean to lay such a heavy burden on his brother. Frankie made up his mind to contact IAM the next day. He was just too tired to deal with anything more. Each time he faced danger he became enormously exhausted. At the moment, all he wanted to do was jump in his warm, toasty bed and sleep for days.

That's exactly what Frankie did. He slept so soundly that by the time he woke up the next morning the family had already left for church. There was a note on the counter from Mom. It read, "Frankie, We decided to go to church and let you sleep in this morning. You looked so worn out when you came home after the music contest last night. I was afraid you were coming down with something. Just rest this morning. You can catch up with us at Granddad's house for lunch. We love you son."

Frankie was glad to be left alone this morning. His thoughts were running rampant. He went upstairs and climbed in the shower. In the middle of showering, he heard IAM'S voice as if it were coming from the running water in the shower head. The voice was so comforting it didn't startle him.

IAM said, "Frankie, I want you to visit the special star tonight at six p.m. Bring your brother, Joe. I shall take away some of your misgivings and fears about the events that have been puzzling your thoughts."

Frankie said, "IAM, you pick the funniest places to communicate." Contemplating IAM's words he finished showering. He dressed in casual clothes and then he walked over to his grandparent's house to wait for the rest of the family.

The young force fighter enjoyed having his grandparents all to himself, without the rest of the family clamoring around. He thought there were times when his grandparent's acted as if they knew something was happening with their grandson. They never confronted him, or spoke a word about it or did anything that might have upset him. That fact alone calmed Frankie, for he didn't discuss any of the supernatural things that were happening in his life with his grandparents. If they did happen to know something was going on, he'd have to chalk it up as another mystery.

CHAPTER 8...
SOARING THE UNIVERSE

Later in the day, Frankie said, Joe would you like to join me in a flight I'm about to embark on? IAM personally invited you to visit the beautiful Rainbow Star.

Joe replied, "I'm not sure I want to go into outer space again. I'll think about."

Later in the day, Joe went up to Frankie and said, Okay, I'll go if we leave around five thirty p.m.

Frankie said, "Okay, thanks Joe."

We walked down the street toward the park. When we were a little ways from home, with no one on the streets, before you could say, "Jackrabbit," Frankie's feathered wings spread out and were zipping straight away into outer space. Once more, it seemed as though it took only a second before we were standing in the middle of the star with dazzling, colored lights flashing and dancing all around them.

There were two chairs and a small table set with yummy looking cookies, small cakes, and a drink that looked like pink lemonade. Although Frankie had warned Joe about the voice, he was startled when he heard it. The voice calmly greeted the boys and asked them to sit down and relax. The first thing IAM did was to calm Joe's racing heart. The voice was so stunning; it was merely a matter of seconds before Joe became unruffled. When he regained his composure, all he could say was, "Wow! Is this for real? Are we actually in the middle of a colored star listening to a voice that sounds like soft rippling water?"

IAM said, "Yes Joe, it's all indubitably real, and so am I. I asked Frankie to bring you here.

"Frankie confided that he's been seeing a man dressed in white and others dressed in red suits during the last few skirmishes he encountered. I understand that you've learned from you're experiences in outer space, that there is a planet called Moonazer. Well there are many other planets in the Universe your unaware of. You're uneducated to the fact, that there is also a spirit world where evil spirits live. Now don't fret, you're not the only ones that don't know. All of mankind is ignorant about the whole realm and scope of all the things the Universe contains. Along with all the occurrences that take place within and around the vastness of time and space that lies beyond the planet earth.

"At this time, Frankie is the only human being with the ability to see the spirits in action as they appear and disappear. The spirits are in reality tormenting and taunting willing victims that leave their soul and heart wide open to commit wickedness. The earth describes it as crime. I describe their deeds as evil iniquity."

IAM went on to explain, "The identities of the men who have started to manifest themselves to Frankie's view are called spirit men or beings. They have the ability to become visible and invisible in the blink of an eye. The man dressed in white with a gold sash around his waist is the leader of the evil spirits. His name is 'NATAS.' The spirit men dressed in red with gold sashes serve Natas. They are his army of followers.

"Frankie, do not fear the Spirit Men. They can't harm you. I've placed a hedge of protection around you. You're going to be a victorious warrior. For your victory is in me. Natas can't touch the people that choose to follow good. Natas asked me to remove the shield of protection I've placed around you. He wants to snuff you out before you've had a chance to use the force fighting abilities that will eventually destroy Natas's evil motives to take more and more humans to his domain.

"Sooner or later, he will try to tempt you. Natas, will try to make you believe that I'm not there. That's why you must never forget. I will never leave either of you to his mercy. Natas has no mercy. He's jealous of every man, woman and child. He's out to destroy as many as he can before he is totally destroyed forever."

Frankie asked, "When would that be?"

IAM said, "That is only for me to know. Commit this lesson to memory. 'Assured victory empowers the army.' Tonight I'm going to take fear out of both your hearts and minds. Your destiny is within my supremacy. My power is greater than Natas or anyone else in the Universe. I created the Universe. It answers to me alone."

After the voice was done reassuring Frankie, he turned his attention to Joe. IAM said, "Joe, feel free to ask any question that's troubling you."

Taking advantage of the opportunity to talk to IAM. Joe said, "I don't

understand why you selected my brother to fight your battles."

IAM replied, "I am, who I am. I choose, whomever it pleases me to choose."

Then Joe asked, "Why did you choose to allow me to know my brother is filled with a force of powers?"

IAM said, "Your brother Frankie needs his own kind to lean on. I've watched you through the years. I know of the deep love you have for you're brother. You're thoughts toward him have been special and precise from the day he was born. Joe, do you recall thinking it was your imagination when you saw a huge bird in the night sky on the eve Frankie was born?"

Joe answered, "Yes. I remember every detail."

IAM said, "The enormous bird you seen that night is the same eagle that soars above Frankie when he fly's in space. Brother Joe, you're a rock of kindness. There are no wicked ways within your heart. That is the reason you were chosen to share Frankie's secret identity. Have I satisfied some of your curiosity?"

"Yes, but there are still so many things I don't understand," Joe said.

IAM remarked, "You have no need to understand at this time. I am the only one in the Universe that has limitless understanding."

Then Joe asked the sixty-four thousand dollar question. "Who are you?"

IAM replied, "All in due time. Someday you'll know the answer. For now, all you need to know is that I am the great 'IAM.' I'm also Joe Stargazers friend. One day, we shall meet again."

Before Joe could say another word, in the twinkling of an eye, IAM whisked the boys back to earth again. They found themselves walking home from the park, just as if they hadn't been in outer space for the past hour.

Just moments before they reached their house, Joe said. "I can't help it, I'm thunderstruck. It's too much to comprehend. But in spite of everything, I feel at peace after talking to IAM and hearing what he had to say. I may not have any answers, but I'm flattered to have a brother that's way beyond cool."

Frankie said, "Thank you Joe for being my friend, as well as my brother."

Leaving it at that, within minutes they we're standing by the front door of their home.

As they walked in the house they both thought of how comforting it was to see Mom and Dad sitting on the sofa, reading the Sunday paper. Both boys went over to where they were seated. They hugged and kissed their parents goodnight, basking in their good fortune to be in a home filled with a loving family. They are the roots that go beyond the realm of time and space.

CHAPTER 9... HOLY COW, WHAT NOW?

Frankie woke up early the next morning and peeked out the window as he had done every morning since he was a tiny tot. He was surprised to see Cynthia strolling across the street to his house so early. He threw on his clothes and bounded down the stairs to answer the door.

Cynthia was distraught and crying. She asked Frankie if he'd come outside and sit on the porch with her for a few minutes.

Frankie asked, "What's up, Cynthia? You never come over this early."

She said, "I need someone to talk to. My parents are splitting up. Mom said she wants to move to another town. I can't stand the thought of not having Mom and Dad together. I don't know what to do."

Frankie sat quietly for a moment, and then said, "Cynthia, don't panic. Maybe they're just having an argument and will change their minds."

She said, "No, they won't. They called me downstairs last night to tell me they were having problems. Dad took his suitcase and left."

Frankie said, "Golly sakes, they've been married for twenty years. Why are they breaking up?"

Cynthia replied, "All I know for sure is that lately they have been feuding quite a bit. Whenever I walk in the room they hush up. My Dad told me he'd be staying at the motel on the outskirts of town. He said anytime I want to talk to him he would be there for me. Before he left, I asked him if it was my fault that he was leaving. Dad cried like a baby. He said, of course not. My sweet daughter, nothing is your fault. Your Mom and I have merely grown apart. It has nothing to do with you." Still, I can't help thinking I must have done something wrong."

Frankie said, "Cynthia, you're one of the sweetest, kindest, nicest girls I know. You've always been obedient to your folks. Whenever I tried to get you to stay out later than the time you were supposed to be home. You said, no, your parents would worry. Heck, there were many times Sam and I stayed out later than we should have and we didn't care if we got in trouble. We were having a good time and didn't want to leave before the rest of the gang. But not you, I had to walk you home right then and there. No dear, Cynthia. I don't believe anything is your fault. Maybe your Mom and Dad will work things out and you won't have to move. I don't know what I'd do without you. You're my special gal. Come on, let's go in the house and find something to eat before we go to school. We have a big day ahead of us today. We have a pep rally before the football game and tonight's the homecoming dance."

Cynthia replied, "How can I possibly think about going to the dance when my life is falling apart?"

Frankie said, "You're going to be with me. I'm going to make sure you have a good time despite the problems between your folks. You have to step back and let your parents work out whatever is between them. You can't do it for them."

She knew in her heart he was right, but it still hurt. Cynthia contemplated the way Frankie treated her so tender and the way he watched over her ever since she could remember. She just couldn't bear to move away and never see him again.

That evening Frankie told his friends it was Cynthia's special night. True to his word, the entire evening he stuck to Cynthia like glue. Although she felt miserable she put up a brave front and kept a smile on her face as much as she possibly could. After the dance was over, Frankie walked Cynthia to the door, kissed her good night, and told her not to worry. He didn't let on how upset he was at the prospect of having his girlfriend move away, let alone seeing her parents split up. Frankie took it for granted that she would always live next door and someday they'd be together for the rest of their life.

As he walked across the street to his house, an idea popped into his head. He talked to his parents a few minutes before going up to bed. The next day, after school, he hopped on his motor scooter and went to visit Cynthia's father at the motel. Mr. Butler answered the door. He was surprised to see Frankie standing there. He said, "Hi Frankie, what brings you here?"

Frankie said, "Mr. Butler, I wonder if I could talk to you?"

"Of course, come in, but please call me Darrell," Mr. Butler said.

Frankie replied, "Okay, thanks Darrell. I know it's none of my business that you're residing in this motel. I came here to see if you'd like to stay in the apartment dad built over the garage. It's vacant right. Mom and Dad both thought you'd be more comfortable living in you're own apartment rather than this tiny room. They said you you've been a friend of the family for a long time and you could stay there rent free as long as you like."

Darrel said, "Well, I do have to admit. I feel a bit cramped in this room. Wouldn't it be a little awkward?"

Frankie replied, "No sir, not in the least. It would be perfect and much more convenient for Cynthia to see you anytime she needs to. No need to tell you how upset and worried she is that you're not living at home. This way, you'll be in the neighborhood and your daughter will feel more secure knowing you're right next door."

Mr. Butler said, "Thank you Frankie. That's so kind of your parents. I think I'll take them up on the offer. I'll get my things together and move in right away. Thanks for not asking me what happened between my wife and I. I'm trying to sort things out. I feel lost without my wife, Carol, but we have some problems I couldn't handle at this time. I can't stand arguing all the time. Our disagreements are not all her fault and until I can figure out what to do, I felt it was best to move out rather than cause more upheavals to my family."

Frankie left the motel and headed for home in a happy mood. He was glad his parents were going to let Mr. Butler live in the apartment over the garage. There was a motive to Frankie's idea. He knew Darrell could look out the window of the apartment and he'd see a full view of his own house across the street from the Stargazer's residence. He parked his scooter and went in to tell his parents that Mr. Butler decided to live in the apartment.

He was bursting to tell everyone the news but when he walked in the house, he could tell something was terribly wrong. Looking forlorn and miserable, Cynthia was sitting across the table from Mom Stargazer. After taking in the scene, Frankie asked, "What's the matter Mom?

Mom said, "Sit down son, we have something to tell you. Mrs. Butler took one too many sleeping pills. She's on her way to the hospital. The ambulance just left. We tried to reach Mr. Butler at the motel, but he wasn't there."

Frankie said, "Oh no! Mom. I just came from seeing him. He's on his way over here. He took you up on the offer to stay in the apartment."

Just then, Mr. Butler pulled in the driveway. They all ran out to tell him his wife was on the way to the hospital.

Mr. Butler didn't say a word. He drove off to the hospital like a mad man.

By the time Darrell arrived at the hospital, his wife was already in the emergency room. The doctors were working frantically to save her life. Several hours went by before he learned that his wife still wasn't out of the woods yet. They wheeled her to a room down the hall to the intensive care unit. Silently weeping, Darrell sat in a chair by her bedside.

Mom and Frankie drove Cynthia to the hospital. When she went into the hospital room and saw the way both of her parents looked so helpless, she fainted and ended up in the bed next to her Mother.

Just as the thought crossed Frankie's mind that this simply can't be happening to his girlfriend and her family, he glanced up. Lo and behold, there stood the man in white, with the glaring python snake eyes. He was standing between the two-hospital beds, laughing at the Butler family's dilemma.

Certain no one else in the room was aware of this spirit being, Frankie forgot himself and uttered loudly, "Get out of here." At the sound of Frankie's voice, the spirit disappeared as quickly as he appeared.

Mrs. Stargazer said, "What did you say Frankie?"

He replied, "Nothing, Mom."

Frankie went over to the window and stared outside. He silently whispered, "IAM, what should I do? I feel helpless." It surprised him when he actually heard IAM'S voice. Not only in his mind, but in his heart as well. It was loud and clear.

The voice of IAM said, "You have the power to heal, not only their bodies but their marriage too. Simply hold their hand a moment, focus your eyes straight into their eyes and they will be made well. Memories of the past hurt will disappear."

Frankie went over to Mr. Butler first and did as he was told. Immediately, Darrell's countenance changed. Then, he stood between the two hospital beds. He held Cynthia and her mother's hand at the same time. In an instant, both of them opened their eyes. Frankie looked deep into their eyes, and instantaneously their entire appearance changed too. For a few moments, the Butlers stared at one another. Straight away, Mr. Butler was on his feet. They were all hugging, and kissing, and telling each other how much they loved one another.

Darrel and his wife held hands and apologized to one another. Mr. Butler said, "I don't know what happened between us but I'll never leave or take my family for granted again. Your all so precious."

Mrs. Butler had to stay in the hospital overnight for observation. The next morning the doctor released her with a clean bill of health. But not before proclaiming Mrs. Butler's recovery was nothing short of a miracle. For when she was first admitted to the hospital her condition was categorized as intensively serious.

The next day Mr. Butler and Cynthia walked into the hospital room to take Mrs. Butler home. The first thing he did was to let his wife know that he loved her. He scooped her in his arms and told her everything was going to be very different.

Mrs. Butler said. "Ditto, Darrell, I love you. I never want to spend another night without you by my side."

Later in the day, Cynthia went over to the Stargazer's home and told Frankie her parents looked and acted like two teen-agers. They walked out of the hospital door arm in arm, gazing into one another's eyes. Something wonderfully miraculous has happened to my parents.

Frankie smiled a knowing smile. He was even amazed that he had power to heal his friends physically and help patch up a marriage on the rocks. He was elated that the Butlers were back together and Cynthia didn't have to move away.

Nevertheless, he remained a little apprehensive about the spirit in white standing in the hospital room smiling gloatingly in the midst of sadness and tragedy. Even though the voice of IAM cautioned him about the spirit world, he still didn't fathom the enormous depth of IAM'S warnings. He couldn't forget the spirit man was laughing, and dancing, and acting as though he was actually willing Mrs. Butler to die. The spirits dancing reminded him of a dance he once saw in a stage play. The name of the play eluded him but he remembered the dancing because it was so sporadic.

He thought about visiting Rainbow Star to ask IAM to tell him more about the spirit world. If he was to right the wrongs of the world, he couldn't just blindly battle the unknown. IAM explained some information about the spirits, but it was a subject he couldn't quite comprehend and he knew so little about. On the other hand, one thing he was sure of was the spirit he encountered in the white suit was the face of pure evil. The spirits had a strange odor about them that seemed to resemble an expensive perfume. The spirit man in white was appearing more and more.

In the meantime, putting the events of the day aside, Frankie got caught up in all the activities he was involved in. At this particular time, he was much to0 busy to make the trip to Rainbow Star, so he put the trip on hold. His busy schedule consisted of working for Mr. Walters, school, playing football, performing in school plays, taking music lessons and playing in a band. With Frankie's full agenda, time was flying by. Things in his life were changing rapidly. Even the town seemed to be moving at a quicker pace. As much as Frankie tried to hide all he was doing to fight crime, his good deeds weren't going unnoticed. The town started to call him "The Samaritan."

Frankie had other things on his mind. He'd be graduating high school in a month and he was getting ready for the graduation ceremony. After graduation his friend, Sam had plans to become a pilot so he'd be moving away. Frankie decided to pursue a career in detective work.

They were making plans hot and heavy one evening when out of the blue Frankie said, "Sam, let's take a break." They went outdoors and sat in the yard. Frankie asked, "Do you remember I once told you I wanted to show you something? Now, don't get shook. I've decided to take you on a journey into outer space."

Sam's mouth flew open but before he could utter a word, Frankie zipped out his wings, slung Sam on his back and off they went whooshing into space. Sam couldn't believe his good fortune. He was living his fantasies, flying among the stars and the planets. Sam looked down at the earth moving further and further away. Before he knew it they were landing on the spectacular planet Moonazer. Despite the fact that Frankie explored several other astounding planets on the way, Moonazer was Sam's favorite.

Sure enough, the moment they landed, Matthew came out to greet them. "It's so nice of you to visit again. What brings you to Moonazer?" Matthew asked.

Frankie said, "Matthew, I want you to meet my best friend. We grew up together. From the time Sam could speak all he ever talked about was flying into outer space. Traveling here tonight is a graduation present to my good buddy. IAM gave me permission to tell him some of my secrets."

Meanwhile, Sam stood awestruck in the midst of the fascinating colors. He was taking in the splendor. Giggling lightheartedly, there was no stopping him. Sam took off his shoes, ran in the thick grass, rolled down a hill and came to a stand still in the middle of the gorgeous flowers. He jumped up and down, whooping and hollering how wonderful it was to be alive. Sam said, "Oh Frankie, what can I say? There's nothing anyone could ever do for me that will compare to the thrill of flying in outer space. I can't believe we're standing on a planet called Moonazer. My God, no one knows this planet even exists!"

Matthew and Frankie laughed at Sam's exuberance. When suddenly, Matthew got a very serious look on his face. Frankie discerned that something was troubling him.

Frankie said, "Matthew is there anything wrong?"

Matthew said, "No. I wouldn't exactly say there is something wrong but I want to share a story with you. I know how concerned you have been about the spirit men you've been seeing. You see my friend, before I lived on Moonazer, there was a time when those very same spirits tempted me. I succumbed to their temptation once. I was very sorry and repentant I allowed myself to be lured into the enticement to commit iniquity against the 'King of King's.' After I was induced that one time to participate in the excitement of the unknown temptation the spirits dangled before me, they wouldn't leave me alone. They kept taunting and tormenting me until IAM rescued me and placed me and my family on this planet where they could never touch me again."

About that time, Matilda and Melinda came out of the house to greet them. Matthew became silent. Frankie had the wisdom not to probe any further.

Matthew introduced Sam to the women and they all went into the house.

They sat down at the table filled with goodies. Sam was beyond excited as he babbled non-stop about his fanciful flight to Moonazer.

After dinner, Matthew gave Sam the tour of the gardens and the fishpond. They were having such a good time but soon it was time to head for home. Matthew and his family said farewell to Frankie and his friend, Sam.

Zoom!!! Boom!!! Before Sam could say a word they were standing in Frankie's room.

Sam said, "Frankie, I'm flabbergasted. I will never forget what you did for me tonight. I want to be a pilot more than ever. Yet, now even that seems tame compared to the experience we had this evening. This day will forever be engraved in my mind and in my heart too. Thank you, for the best graduation present ever. I'm so pumped I don't know why I feel so exhausted at the same time. I know we still have a lot to discuss about our plans for graduation day but could we wait and talk about them tomorrow morning?"

Frankie knew why Sam was exhausted. After every trip he took into outer space, Frankie felt the same overpowering tiredness. The boy's nodded off instantly.

Graduation day arrived and went off without a hitch. After the commencement ceremony, Sam presented Frankie a huge gift-wrapped package. Frankie tore off the paper. To his amazement, it was a breathtaking painting of the stars and the planet Moonazer. The painting was unlike anything anyone had ever seen. Everyone asked Sam where he got the idea to paint something so unique. They were enthralled and couldn't take their eyes off the beautiful work of art.

The magnolia trees and rolling hills looked exact. The colors were vibrantly fantastic. They seemed to jump out of the picture. Sam was a talented photographer and artist acquainted with just the right colors to enhance his artwork and photographs.

Joe and Greg knew exactly where Sam got the idea for the painting. They were awestruck by the beauty he captured on canvas. Frankie thanked Sam and told him the painting would be part of his life forever. He hung the painting over the fireplace in the front room.

No one ever walked into the Stargazer's home without commenting on the exquisiteness of the painting. Of course, not knowing planet Moonazer was a real place and Sam's inspiration for the unique work of art, people merely thought it was a creation of Sam's vivid imagination.

With graduation over Frankie decided to move into his own apartment. He found a place close to his parent's home. Naturally, Kylee dog had to move in with him.

The apartment building had an extra room he could use to start his own investigative business. Cynthia took on the responsibility of being his secretary. Frankie was in seventh heaven having her near him all day long. He hoped to marry her someday in the near future.

Everyone that knew Frankie thought he would go with Sam to pursue a career as a pilot or at least check out a new space program the government was starting. The program was attracting a lot of young men. Frankie never gave up his love of wanting to be a pilot. Even though he had his very own secret flight excursions and adventures, he decided to take private flying lessons on his days off and he continued attending a local college. He was determined to get a law degree too.

After he opened his own private detective business, it wasn't long before the phone began to ring off the hook. Frankie was only eighteen but he was on his way to becoming self-sufficient. His deeds were well known among local police and politicians, he was soon branching out further and further into crime fighting scenes in the big city of "Levid." It wasn't long before the Governor asked Frankie to work for the entire state on some of the unsolved cases. He offered to put Frankie on a retainer. It didn't seem to matter that he was fresh out of high school. His reputation as a crime fighter was intact at a young age. It was literally impossible for some of his rescues to go unnoticed.

One evening shortly after Frankie opened his own business, he was in his office doing some paperwork when he heard a loud crash. Seconds later, the Walter's chauffer, Don, burst into his office. Hysterical and crying he asked Frankie to come to the airport right away. Mr. and Mrs. Walters have been in a terrible plane crash that exploded before it got off the ground.

Frankie whizzed to the scene in seconds but he was to late. Their private plane was in flames. The only thing he could do was put out the fire and pull the charred bodies out of the remains of the tragic flight. He was devastated. He loved the Walters as if they were his own parents. The entire town mourned the loss of the Walters and the pilot. The memorial service and funeral was one of the largest gatherings the town had ever seen.

The Stargazer family was bereaved. They became such good friends with the Walters they could hardly stand the thought of not having them to fellowship with anymore. Don played "Amazing Grace" on the bagpipes and there wasn't a dry eye in the church. Since there were no living relatives, the Stargazers took care of all the arrangements and served the crowd refreshments in the church basement. Most everyone in town pitched in and brought food to the church.

After the mourners left and the cleanup work was done the Stargazer's took several plates of food and went to Grandma and Grandpa's house. They were feeling poorly and couldn't attend the services.

After the funeral, Frankie couldn't stand the thought of spending the night

alone. He walked over to his apartment and picked up Kylee. He wanted to spend the night in his old room at his parents' house.

The Stargazers invited Don to spend the night at their place too. The poor man seemed to be in a daze the entire day. He felt comforted by their sympathy and accepted their offer. Mom pulled out the sofa bed and gave him a pair of dad's pajamas to wear.

After everyone settled down for the night, Frankie went out on the roof for a few minutes. He couldn't seem to clear his head of the painful shock he still felt since the tragic accident. The events of the last three days took their toll. Kylee sensed Frankie's sadness and she snuggled close to him. He patted the dog's head and said, "Good old Kylee. I love you faithful friend."

Several days after the funeral, an attorney from the city called 'Levid,' came to see Frankie. He introduced himself as Tyrone Trevor. Tyrone said, "Frankie, I'm a very old friend of the Walters. I'm sure you're aware that Mr. and Mrs. Walters had no living relatives. They were very fond of you and your family."

Frankie replied, "Yes, but what does that have to do with me?"

The attorney replied, "I have a copy of the Walters' will. They left everything to you. Except for the guesthouse in back of their house and a trust fund they left for Don. They made sure he'd have a home and a pension to live on for the rest of his life."

Staring at the attorney, Frankie said, "I don't understand. Why would they leave everything to me? I know the Walter's were very charitable and supported various aid organizations for many years. There are so many worthy charities they could have left the money to."

Tyrone said, "It seems that Mr. and Mrs. Walters left the decision up to you Frankie. I'll explain everything. If you choose to use my services, I can continue to work for you in the same manner I worked for the Walters."

After hours of unbelievable conversation with the attorney, Frankie walked over to his parent's house to tell his mom and dad the news. Although they were thrilled for their son, a worried look came across their faces.

Dad said. "Frankie, I think you're a little too young to take on all the projects you intend to accomplish. How can you possibly handle the enormous ventures?"

Frankie remarked, "Mom and Dad, you need to stop looking at me like I'm still a little boy falling on my bum in the back yard. I'm not going to attempt to do anything by myself. Tyrone will set the plans in motion.

"I intend to hire Joe and Greg to work with Tyrone. They won't have to work as a sales clerk ever again. They will be in charge of helping others. While they are helping others, they will be blessed with more prosperity than they ever imagined possible.

"Greg is good with children so I'm putting him in charge of changing the Walters' estate into a home for the homeless children living on the streets. It will be a home for children who feel trapped to live in hopeless situations. Greg will have the freedom to hire as many people as it takes to achieve this goal. Joe can be in charge of bookkeeping and handle the finances. Tyrone will be in charge of the legal work and all the different charities we intend to set up. It's a big project to undertake, but one that's needed. The Walters' left enough finances to take care of several homes. We can open one here and we'll open several homes in Levid. There's enough money in the estate to provide proper clinical needs too. We will definitely make sure each child is handled on an individual basis and given the tender loving care they deserve."

CHAPTER 10…
THE FORCE FIGHTER'S CRUSADE

With the plans intact for the "TLC Home for Children," the Stargazer boys began the crusade to provide a place to the homeless orphans. The Walters mansion was ready to provide rooms to ten children. The building in the city of Levid was almost finished. It would house up to thirty children of all ages, including unwanted abandoned babies.

Frankie hired Don, to help with the children's homes. Don's first order of business was to check with the mayor and request that the newly formed organization, "TLC," be considered a safe haven for children. Don informed the city officials they would provide homes to children they picked up off the street, children that had no one to care for him or her and nowhere to go. The TLC organization has no restrictions as to race, color or creed. All children were welcome. The TLC initials stood for "Tender Loving Care."

The TLC association hired a staff that consisted of doctors, counselors, nurses, orderlies, maintenance people and bodyguards. They were to keep the children safe from harm and from each other until they received proper care and were taught to get along in a home environment.

They made sure the rooms were sunny and cheerful. Each child would have his or her own private area, including its own bathroom. The boy's rooms were painted in light shades of blue and white. The girl's rooms were painted in pastel pink and white. The dressers were filled with new clothes, toiletries, school supplies and everything the children needed to start their new life.

Frankie provided each room with a small radio. He remembered what a luxury a radio used to be when his family couldn't afford to buy one. Frankie recalled how much he and his brothers and sisters enjoyed the tiny little crystal set they saved all summer to purchase. It wasn't practical to supply each room with a TV set so they placed TV sets in two of the rooms they fixed into lounges. The children could relax in a quiet atmosphere.

The news about the homes opening traveled quickly. It wasn't long before both homes were full. Greg wanted to add more rooms on to the Walters house to provide space for ten more children. The newly formed organization was surprised at the unwanted children that were living on the streets, right in their own hometown. They expanded the program to include pregnant teens that had been thrown out of their homes.

Many of the town's people wanted to donate to the home. Frankie gladly allowed the donations to pour in. As the organization grew so did the board members. With donations pouring in, TLC members were anxious to expand their ministry to include homes for the elderly that had very little income to live on. The organization wanted to provide the elderly with the medical care they needed and couldn't afford on the small pensions they tried to get by on, and doing without the barest necessities.

Between Joe, Greg, Frankie, Don, and Tyrone the newly formed crew accomplished all they set out to do within the year. Now that things were running smoothly, Frankie decided to let Joe, Greg, Don and Tyrone handle everything as he set out to pursue his career in the detective business.

In the meantime, Frankie's best friend, Sam, was in the air force and was coming to Blue Rivers for the weekend. After graduation, they became busy as bees and hadn't seen each other in a long while. It was going to be fun just to hang out and reminisce about old times.

Mom and Dad were planning a celebration Friday evening to honor the boy's accomplishments. They invited Sam's parents to join the festivities. Mom was cooking the children's favorite foods. Angela and Lynn were helping prepare the meal when Sam and Frankie arrived. Lynn blushed when Sam greeted her. They'd been writing steadily since Sam left town. They didn't have to tell anyone they were crazy about each other. It was written all over their face when they saw one another.

Frankie teased Sam saying, "You old son of a gun! How long has this been going on?"

"What on earth are you talking about?" Sam asked.

Frankie laughingly said, "I'm surprised I'm the last to know that my best friend has a secret crush on my sister. I remember the way you used to protect Lynn from the big bad wolves in town. I didn't suspect it was because you were one of them and you wanted Lynn for yourself."

Sam blushed. Between his and Lynn's red face, you could light up a room. They laughed and carried on a bit longer. Then Frankie went into the front room to talk to Dad.

Dad Stargazer was a quiet man. It didn't matter what the subject was about. When Dad spoke it was with such wisdom it commanded everyone's attention.

A few minutes later, Joe, Greg, and Don came in the door with Grandma and Grandpa Stargazer.

Frankie said, "It sure feels good to be sitting with the entire family and my best friend. We've all been so busy the past year I didn't realize how much I missed all of us being together in the same room at one time. I enjoy the feeling of being surrounded by loved ones talking, laughing and reminiscing."

After supper they adjourned from the dining room and went back into the living room. Mom set a huge pot of coffee and every kind of dessert imaginable on the coffee table so they could just relax and enjoy one another's company.

Frankie didn't want the evening to end. His joy was short lived. It all started when Sam and Lynn decided to go for a walk. Several minutes later they came running into the house to tell everyone about a hullabaloo that was taking place in the downtown area. There was a woman standing on the very edge of the hotel roof and she was about to jump off. The fire and police department were trying to talk her into climbing back into the hotel window. She just stood on the ledge and didn't say a word. She was ready to throw her life away if anyone came near her.

Frankie raced out of the house and zoomed to the troubled area. He flinched as he viewed spirit beings dressed in red suits with bright gold sashes around their waist standing next to the woman. They were circling around her enticing her to jump. When the spirits saw Frankie approaching, they vanished.

Acting quickly, Frankie stretched out his hand and froze everyone in time. He flew up to the top of the building to rescue the woman so fast she didn't know what happened. All of a sudden, she was standing on the ground with Frankie's arms around her. In a flash, he unfroze the people standing in the streets.

No one knew what really took place. Sometimes, people just surmise a situation and assume whatever they feel like assuming, no matter how things look. It didn't matter much what they assessed during the times Frankie lends a helping hand to those in need. The presuming conversation between the crowds of people went on and on. The fire department took credit for catching the woman in the net they held and the police claimed they were responsible for rescuing her.

In the meantime, Frankie asked the woman if she wanted to go to the hospital.

She said, "No." Then she started to panic.

Frankie soothingly calmed her down. After she settled down, he said, "Let's just walk to my parent's home. We can talk there."

On the way to his house, Frankie asked what her name was. The woman didn't answer. He wondered what could possibly be so bad that it would entice her to take her own life?

After they walked a few blocks, she spoke in a voice barely audible. All she would say was that her name was Kathleen.

When they reached his parent's home, she asked if she could sit on the porch swing while she caught her breath. Frankie obliged her and they sat quietly. Mrs. Stargazer came out to the porch and asked them to come inside, but Kathleen refused. Mom told her son to leave her and Kathleen alone for a few minutes.

Mother sat on the swing and gently held Kathleen in her arms. She talked so serenely, in a few minutes they both came in the house. Mom sat Kathleen at the kitchen table. She fixed her a cup of hot coffee and put a plate of food in front of her. At first, Kathleen hesitated. Then she ate every morsel of food Mom placed before her. Mom was the greatest. Not only did she have Kathleen eating her food, she had Kathleen eating out of her hand too. Mom talked Kathleen into taking a bath and putting on some of Lynn's clean clothes. The woman was so thin and pale. Mom helped her up the stairs and ran her a bath. She told Kathleen she'd wait on the window seat at the end of the upstairs hallway. Mom gasped when Kathleen finally stepped out of the bathroom. She said, "For goodness sakes! You're just a child."

Kathleen said, "Yes maam, I'm only seventeen. I put on my sister's clothes and all that make up so I could look older."

When they went back downstairs, the family was astounded to see the transformation that had taken place in the bathroom. Mom said, "I'd like to introduce you all to Kathleen." Everyone made over her and she started to feel comfortable in the midst of so much love. Kathleen had never been around a family like the Stargazers. No one had ever treated her with such compassion. All she'd ever been subjected to was heartache and hard times.

After a few minutes everyone decided to leave for home and the Stargazers were left alone with Kathleen. She surprised them by speaking

Kathleen said, "I'm sorry for interrupting the party. I feel I owe you an explanation. I don't want to infringe on you but I have no money and no place to go. I felt desperate tonight, but there's one thing I'm certain of. I didn't intend to kill myself when I walked up to the roof of the hotel. I was just going to spend the night there and try to figure out what to do next. Then something strange happened. One minute I was sitting on the rooftop in the middle of the building, staring at the lights of the city. All of a sudden, I was standing on the edge of the roof. It felt as if someone was pushing and goading me to destroy myself. I can't explain how I could have been standing on the roof one moment and the next moment I was standing on the ground with Frankie embracing and comforting me."

Mother said, "Kathleen, you're going to stay here with us tonight. My sons are in charge of housing homeless children. In the morning, the boys will find you a place to live in one of the TLC homes. We can work out the details tomorrow. Rest assured, tonight, you're in the house of people that care about what happens to you. We will make sure you have a place to stay and a chance to get a decent job."

Tears of relief poured from Kathleen's eyes. She was so thankful. She asked, "Am I in the home of Angels?"

Mom said, "Not by a long shot. We are just plain ordinary folks that make mistakes and have problems too. But we have one another. We know how hard it is for people that have no one in the world to turn to." Mom took Kathleen by the hand and led her up to Frankie's old bedroom and actually sang her a song and tucked her in bed.

After things calmed down, Sam and Frankie decided to bid everyone adieu. They headed for Frankie's apartment with Kylee running between their feet all the way home.

After they had walked a few steps, Sam remarked, "Whew! We had quite a night. Hey buddy?"

"We sure did," Frankie replied. "Gosh almighty! Lately it seems as if there is always something happening. On a lighter note, I've just got to ask you Sam. How serious is it between you and my sister Lynn?"

Sam said, "I love Lynn. Someday I want to ask her to be my wife. I've had my eye on her for a very long time. Lynn's the only gal for me. She's the prettiest girl in the town of Blue Rivers. Oops! Maybe I should say that she ties for first place with your girlfriend, Cynthia."

CHAPTER 11 ...
THE COURSE OF SPACE EVENTS

Frankie and Sam still had all day Saturday to hang out together and catch up on old times. As they were contemplating on what they were gong to do, Frankie asked Sam if he would like to go on an adventure.

Sam's eye's lit up as he said, "Try and stop me Frankie boy. I'm ready and raring to go."

"That's great," Frankie replied. "Let's have breakfast with Cynthia and then we'll take off. I have to let her know I won't be around all day. I'm sure she'd love to have a day off too."

The next morning Sam was bowled over when he saw the cool blue convertible car Frankie purchased to cruise around in. He threw the keys at Sam and said, "Give it a go buddy, then swing by and pick up Cynthia. You can chauffeur us to our favorite restaurant."

After they arrived at the diner and were seated, Frankie told Cynthia he'd be gone all day. He was aware of the way everyone questioned Cynthia when they couldn't find him. She was the one person that usually knew where he was. They had a good time laughing and talking during breakfast. Afterwards, the boys dropped Cynthia off at her house and parked the car by Frankie's apartment.

Frankie said, "Sam, before I tell you where we're going, let's go up to my apartment for a few minutes before we take off."

"You do realize that you're being mysterious," Sam remarked.

Frankie merely smiled.

They were in the apartment for just a few minutes before they were racing one another down the stairs and out the door. In a matter of seconds, they were speeding off into outer space.

Sam had an idea that's what Frankie had in mind but with Frankie you just never knew for sure. Sam was elated as they wheeled in and out of the cosmos. He couldn't stop thinking of how amazing it was to have a friend like Frankie.

Frankie had the power to simply touch Sam and his entire being was able to change so he could handle breathing and flying though space without any ill effects. Sam wasn't the least bit afraid. Sam knew nothing could harm him while he was with Frankie. It wasn't long before they reached planet Moonazer. Once again, Matthew was waiting to greet them.

Frankie said, "How do you know the exact second we set foot on you're planet?

Matthew said, "I can't tell you. Now, to what do I owe the pleasure of this visit?"

"I need to ask you for a favor," Frankie replied.

Mathew said, "Sure Frankie, but first I have a new pony to show off. It was born this morning."

The three of them walked into the barn. There stood the most stunning pony. It was standing under its mother's legs, sucking milk. It was white with brown and black spots that looked like tiny little hearts.

Frankie said, "The pony is beautiful. Everything on Moonazer is fantastic. I love it here. It's so relaxing. Sometimes I dream about living here and simply sitting under the magnolia trees, doing absolutely nothing. Of course, I'd want my girl, Cynthia, to be right here beside me."

Grinning from ear to ear, Matthew said, "Well Frankie maybe someday, you can do just that."

Frankie said, " Matthew, can Sam stay with you for just a short time while I make a trip to Rainbow Star? I need to talk to IAM."

Sam asked, "Why can't I go with you, Frankie?"

Frankie said, "I don't have permission to take you along with me. I promise I won't be gone too long."

Sam replied, "All right Frankie. As long as Matthew doesn't mind putting up with me."

Matthew remarked, "I'd consider it an honor and a pleasure to spend time with you Sam."

With that, Frankie took off and went soaring to his destination. The voice of IAM greeted him the moment he landed on Rainbow Star. IAM said, "I know why you're here. I'm cognizant of your troubled feelings at the sight of spirit men enticing humans. You're not quite sure why they are there, or why they disappear the moment they see you. The spirits fear you at this time. They haven't learned how to destroy who you are. They have no idea what they could use to overpower love and goodness in your heart.

"As yet, only their leader NATAS is surmising where your force over them comes from. They overpower human beings that reveal their weaknesses. The spirit beings can only tempt and use people that succumb to their temptations and their version of wickedness, evil, sorcery and witchcraft.

"You're aware of the black planet called 'Nomed,' where the evil spirits live. What you're not aware of is the spirits have access to visit the earth anytime they choose. It's imperative to understand, if there were only one human being on the face of the earth with evil intent in their heart, the spirits would still have access to penetrate the planet. That's all it takes. Just one wicked and immoral person can open the door for many evil spirits to enter earth's atmosphere.

"As you know, there are quite a few humans with evil intent and malice toward others. The love they have for themselves and their own selfish motives invite the spirit beings to have a hey day on planet earth.

"Matthew explained why the spirit men couldn't penetrate his planet due to the seal of safe protection they have around it. Therefore, there is no evil on Moonazer. But what the people of Moonazer are not aware of is that the secret to the protective seal is within their own hearts. That's one of the keys that prevents NATAS and his army of spirits from penetrating certain planets. They can't enter a place where every one lives in peace and harmony, and who have no ill thoughts or malevolence within.

"Where your heart is so also is your treasure. If evil iniquity were not in someone's heart, it would not be in his or her mind either. Be on guard, for the spirits are testing and taunting you each time they reveal themselves. They're looking for something to destroy you with.

"One day, the spirit Natas and his followers are planning to attack Earth. The only reason they haven't succeeded in doing so already is because they are trying to entice more and more humans to serve by their wicked side."

Frankie asked, "What do you mean serve by their side?"

IAM said, "The human beings the spirits have in their clutches choose to be used. They have given themselves over to Natas with their own free will.

Humans have one of two choices. There's no middle ground. One choice is to choose to serve the light. The other is choosing to serve darkness. Someday, the spirits on the dark planet will attack the earth in full force. Before that day happens, Natas is out to recruit as many evil people as he can to join his army. One day, the spirits will be sealed from harming mankind. But until then, Natas will continue to obliterate all those he has access to. Whoever joins his army will be thrown on the Black Planet."

Frankie replied, "Gee Whiz, IAM! This all sounds like something out of a science fiction horror story. What's going to happen to all the people? If such a mighty battle's about to take place on planet earth, won't that destroy the whole universe?"

IAM said, "That's possible. There are skirmishes that take place on your planet every second of the day."

Frankie said, "I need you to spell out what you're trying to tell me."

IAM replied, "Spirits battle for the minds of humans. They never rest. When one spirit becomes weak or tired or if they can't find a way to infiltrate their mind, they have another spirit ready to take their place. When one temptation doesn't work, they use another temptation to temp humans with.

"The spirits lie, kill, steal, creep, crawl, sneak and peek at all they can make use of. They utilize whatever it takes to break down and decay the moral values of mankind. It's not a pretty picture to envision.

"Don't be dismayed when the time comes. You will know exactly what to do with the force of power that it will take to destroy the spirit men. At this point in time the spirits are playing games. In due time, they won't be able to elude you with their vanishing act."

A little stymied, Frankie remarked, "Some of what your telling me is like trying to solve a puzzle but the pieces don't fit. I don't understand it."

IAM said, "Have patience. One day you will understand. You're going to lead armies of men who enlist in the army of the light. Do not dismay." In a flash, the voice ended the conversation and Frankie found himself back in Moonazer sitting on one of the stone chairs next to Sam and Matthew.

Sam remarked, "Fancy meeting you here, Frankie. I swear if I live to be 5,000 years old, I'll never get used to your fast entries and exits."

"Sam, I hate to hit and run but its time to leave," Frankie said.

Matthew asked, "What's your hurry?"

Frankie said, "I want to check something out." As quickly as they arrived, the boys were speedily on their way back to earth. Frankie wanted to see if he could find the black planet and observe where the spirit men lived. He knew he couldn't land on the planet but sometimes curiosity got the best of him.

On the way home, he took his time seeing sights he hadn't seen on the previous flights he'd been on. Several times he spotted a few spirits. He tried to follow them to their destination. However once again, just as quickly they appeared, they vanished into thin air. He thought it was weird, the spirits acted as if they didn't see him.

Frankie never found the location of the dreaded Black Planet and eventually he headed straight for earth. Along the way, he saw a purple colored planet he hadn't noticed before. He made a mental note to explore it sometime.

As soon as Sam and Frankie had their feet on the ground, they headed to the Stargazer's house. Sometimes when Frankie came back to earth from outer space, he had the urge to see his Mom and Dad. When he spotted his parents sitting on the porch swing, his cares and worries seemed to fade.

There was something so serene about seeing his parents sitting together, holding hands. It made him feel safe and secure to be in their presence. Frankie and Sam greeted them, and asked how Kathleen was doing.

Mom said, "Kathleen is going to spend another night here. At the moment, she's not home. Joe took her to a movie."

Before heading back to Frankie's apartment they went into the house to raid the refrigerator.

The next morning, Sam thanked Frankie for the exciting space trip and hospitality. Then he left for the Air Force Base. Along the way, Sam couldn't help thinking it seemed tame to fly a plane after cruising the Universe.

Oh, how Sam would love to tell the other pilots about his adventures in outer space. He knew he never would betray his friend's confidence. Besides, along with his promise to keep his friend's activities a secret, Sam knew everyone would think he was crazy. He'd be the laughing stock of his company.

During his fantastic, adventurous travels with his friend, Sam was getting an idea to design and build a rocket ship. It would be a beautiful rocket ship that could travel through outer space and visit other planets. Although there were scientists working on a space program, Sam had an insight into space flying the top brass weren't aware of. The design had to include suits that would accommodate human needs to breathe in space. He knew he would have died in outer space if not for Frankie's awesome powers that allowed him to breathe safely.

It was tremendous zooming in and out of the planets and stars even though there were asteroids hurling all about Sam knew he was never in harm's way when he was with Frankie. Sam was bursting to tell Frankie about the rocket ship and the other ideas he had. But first, he wanted to work it out down to the last detail. Driving back to the air base, Sam contemplated the way he'd draw the designs with intricate details showing how the rocket would look and the way it would work. In the meantime, Sam had to be content with piloting airplanes.

CHAPTER 12…
FRANKIE BATTLES THE PYTHON GANG & WITCHES

The moment Frankie strode into his office, Cynthia handed him a note from the Governor. After he read it, Frankie told Cynthia that he had to leave right away. She was to call his folks and tell them he'd be back in a few days.

Frankie arrived at the State Office and headed straight into the Governor's office.

Governor Rick said, "Hello Frankie. I'm glad to see you. I'm sorry this is such short notice but something came up that requires immediate attention. "

Frankie replied, "I came as soon as I got your message. What's up Governor?"

The Governor said, "I need someone I can trust to investigate. We believe Senator Gray met with foul play. No one has a clue as to why he was targeted. The Senator had a spotless record. There could be more to the case than meets the eye.

"It was no accident. Someone rigged Senator Gray's car with a homemade bomb device. A few months ago, the same type of bomb was used to kill a member of a gang called the 'Pythons.' The incident was rigged to look as if someone other than the members or the gang had anything to do with the crime. No one was arrested. The Python members keep their nose clean and avoid confrontations with police. They act innocent and cooperative. They're always willing to help the police clear up cases we can't get to first base solving.

"The Pythons eluded questioning by the FBI during an investigation that's taking place right now. It has to do with the disappearance of a Hollywood movie star that was visiting the city of Levid for the grand opening of his new film. We managed to keep his disappearance quiet so far. It won't be long before the news media gets wind of actor, Rayven Delano's disappearance. The reporters have started nosing around.

"Now, Frankie, you don't have to take the case if you don't want to. It will be risky and may take more than a few days. You 'd have to go undercover within the midst of the gang. We need to find out everything we can to stop them from committing more crimes. I've asked you to handle the case because you're young enough to get by with infiltrating the organization.

"No one has been able to touch the Pythons. They cover their behinds with their willingness to help local officials and with due process of law that says they are innocent until proven guilty. The gang's involvement is a personal gut feeling I have. No one could know as much as the pythons do and be as familiar with the details of each case if they didn't know exactly what was happening before the law was called to the scene of the crime. I think they're involved or connected in some manner to most of the unsolved cases we've had to deal with in the past few years."

"I wasn't expecting a job of this magnitude," Frankie said.

Governor Rick replied, "It won't be easy to infiltrate their territory or participate with the members. No one seems to know what goes on in the meetings they hold almost nightly within the walls of an enormous building they bought on the east side of town.

"The Pythons named the building 'THE NATAS.' They remodeled every room in the ten-story building. They keep the entire four-block area looking like Park Avenue.

"Aside from wearing leather jackets with the name Python engraved on the sleeve, the men and women that belong to the gang don't wear the usual gang garb. They're not only well dressed, they're well versed. Most of the members come from decent hard working, law-abiding citizens that have never been in trouble."

Frankie wondered why the building was called the Natas. It was the same name IAM called the handsome spirit man. After a few minutes Frankie said, "Okay Governor. I'll do it. How long will it take to brief me, and who do I contact if I learn something you should know right away?"

Several officers briefed Frankie as well as they could with the knowledge they had thus far on the gang's procedures. Their actions and activities in the community was not the usual gang activity. The Pythons held dances for the local youth, put on theatrical plays, and were involved in community functions. They were always the first to volunteer for charitable causes. However even though they talked and looked like Joe College there was something phony about the entire scenario.

Governor Rick said, "I'm sure I don't have to warn you to be careful. If you see they're getting suspicious, get out of their midst as fast as you can. As innocent as they act and come across, they are capable of playing very rough. Be on your guard at all times. Don't confide anything of consequence to any of the members. Most of all, don't forget no matter how friendly they act, the Pythons will turn on you in a hot minute.

"When you walk through their doors you will be totally alone in the enemy's camp. We don't want to cause suspicion. Therefore, the police won't be able to drive around the building any more than they usually do."

Frankie called Cynthia and told her he'd be gone a little longer than expected and he wasn't free to tell her the reason why. He didn't waste any time. He hung up the phone and went straight into the heart of Python territory. He wandered up and down a few streets a long while before he headed for the restaurant the Python members were known to hang out in.

The instant Frankie set foot inside the café, he spotted several members wearing leather jackets with the Python emblem on the sleeve. He sat at a table directly across from them and struck up a conversation. The pythons were amicable. It only took a few moments before the gang members asked Frankie to join them at their table. Frankie ambled over to their table and said, "I'm new in town. I was wondering if you could recommend an inexpensive place I could rent a room for a few days?"

They introduced themselves as Fred and Gene. The two men tried not to be too obvious as to what their motives were. Gene said, " Where are you from?"

Frankie replied, "I'm from Fayetteville. It's about four hundred miles from here." Seemingly satisfied with Frankie's answers, Gene said, " There's a hotel that rents small apartments located around the corner from the café.

Frankie asked Fred and Gene, "Do you happen to know where I can find a job around here?"

What kind of work are you looking for?" Fred asked.

The young investigator said, "I don't care what kind of job it is, as long as I can make a few dollars."

"If you're interested, we might be able to help you find a job," Fred said.

Frankie replied, Thank you. I'm beat. I'd like to check into a hotel.

Gene said, "We'll walk you to the hotel and help you get a room."

The hotel clerk was neatly dressed. He had on a suit, a white shirt, and a tie. He was extremely friendly. The clerk seemed to know Fred and Gene.

Fred said, "Would you fix Frankie up with an apartment suite." The clerk winked at them.

Fred said, "Frankie, we need to take off. We'll be in touch with you real soon."

The clerk gave Frankie a key to room forty and asked for a month's rent in advance. Without a word, Frankie paid him and went up to the tiny apartment. The last thoughts he had before falling asleep were centered on the events of the evening and the way he seemed to gain Gene and Fred's confidence so quickly. It seemed much too easy.

Early the next morning there was a knock on the door. Still sleepy eyed, Frankie got up and opened the door. It was Fred and Gene.

They said, "Come on lazy bones, daylight's burning. We have a proposition to offer you."

"Give me a minute to shower and get dressed." Frankie said.

When Frankie finished dressing, he walked back into the room where Fred and Gene were waiting for him. Frankie said, "This is so sudden. I thought it would take a lot longer than this to find a job. What kind of job is it?"

It's a surprise," Gene said.

They left the hotel. As they walked down the sidewalk, Frankie noticed Fred and Gene both had a sly smile plastered on their face. They only had to walk a short ways before they came to a place called, 'The Natas Building.' Upon entering, he observed a receptionist in the front office. A few cleaning men were scrubbing floors in a huge hallway.

His newfound friends escorted him to an office several steps down the hall. Inside the door stood a clean cut man. He was tall, dark and handsome and he appeared to be around thirty years old. He looked the part of a well-groomed successful business executive. Gene introduced Frankie to Gentry. He was obviously the head of the Python's organization.

Gentry said, "Good to meet you, Frankie. I hear you're the new kid on the block. Are you looking for a job?"

Frankie said, "Yes. I'm new in town. I need a job real bad. I have enough to live on for several weeks. If I don't find a job right away, I'll have to move on."

Gentry looked Frankie over real good. Then he asked him, "How would you like to work for me?"

"That depends. What sort of work are we talking about?" Frankie asked.

Gentry said, "I need someone to help collect rent money every month. The job takes three days a week. You would be earning the same amount of money as if you had worked five days."

Frankie asked, "You mean to say, all I have to do is collect money from people that owe you and that's it?"

"That's exactly right," Gentry said. "Then he went on to explain the routine. When Gentry was finished talking, once again, he asked Frankie if he was interested.

Frankie replied, "I'd be a fool not to be interested. When do I start?"

Gentry said, "You can start tomorrow. Fred and Gene, will show you the ropes today."

"Okay. Thanks." Frankie replied.

On the way out, Gene said, "Let's get some breakfast before we make the rounds." They went to the same restaurant where they had met the night before and devoured huge plates of eggs and pancakes.

Gene explained, "The job is easy. All you have to do is walk down one side of the street then up the other side for several blocks and collect rent money from the business places that have the small letter G in the right hand corner of the window.

Curious, Frankie asked, "How did Gentry come to own so much property?"

Gene said, "Gentry is an only child. His mom and dad both died in a car accident. Gentry inherited all their property."

After they finished eating breakfast, Fred and Gene showed Frankie the routine. They walked in one store after another collecting money. A few business owners seemed apprehensive when the Pythons came into their establishment. But they were congenial and friendly. They introduced Frankie and told the proprietors Frankie would be collecting the rent from now on.

After spending the whole day with the two Python members, Frankie simply wanted to go back to the hotel and crash. Gene and Fred insisted that Frankie come with them to a party. They said they wanted him to meet some of their friends.

Tiredly, Frankie ended up saying, "Sure, that would be fine." Nevertheless, he continued to wonder why the python members didn't seem the least bit worried about trusting him so rapidly. Frankie rehashed the way it was all going to fast too soon. The two men didn't act concerned. They didn't give any indication toward the fact that Frankie could possibly be an undercover agent.

Fred and Gene hurriedly walked with Frankie to the Natas Building. As they entered through the front door, Frankie noticed that they each had a key to the place. There was no one around. He merely assumed everyone was through working for the day.

They walked up a flight of stairs to the second floor and stepped into an apartment that looked like a showcase out of House Beautiful. Gene said, "Welcome to our humble living quarters." He opened the refrigerator, got a beer for himself and handed one to Frankie.

Fred said, "By the way, Frankie, I forgot to tell you that we're going to have supper in just a little while. A few of our friends are going to bring some delicious food over."

"This is one of the most beautiful apartments I've ever seen," Frankie remarked.

Fred said, "When Gentry remodeled the building, he decided to construct the upstairs floors into apartments. He hired a famous decorator to design each living quarters with a different theme. Gentry has a penthouse on the top floor. He will be joining us soon to ask how your first day on the job went."

About half an hour later the doorbell started to ring. People showed up with every imaginable kind of food. The enormous room was filling up fast. Frankie assumed most of the people were gang members. Governor Rick was right. They didn't look like the average gang that hung out on street corners. Everyone was well dressed and they all seemed to be very affluent. They looked as if they should be living in a college dormitory.

One of the men started to play a baby grand piano located in an adjoining room. Several people started singing. There was a real shindig starting to take place. It wasn't long before Gentry came strolling in with a pretty woman on his arm. He greeted Frankie, and then he introduced his woman friend as Lisa.

Fred and Gene acted so nonchalant, like it was no big deal to have a few friends over to meet him. However, their motive for having the party was to find out what Frankie was doing in Python territory. Frankie hadn't gotten by with anything.

Lisa talked to Frankie for a short time and then she asked, "Frankie, what to you think about witchcraft and sorcery? Do you think it's a figment of people's imagination or do you think it's real?"

Everyone in the room suddenly got very quiet. All eyes focused on Frankie.

Frankie replied, "I don't know what to think about it. The subject of witchcraft never came up before."

Lisa said, "I'm a real witch. Do I look like one?"

"No. I don't think you look like a witch." Frankie replied.

Gentry changed the subject. He said, "Frankie, we took you into our confidence, set you up with a job, and a place to live. Now, it's your turn to take us into your trust. Tell us how you came to be in the area?"

Once more, Frankie repeated that he had no home or family to tie him down. He merely wandered from town to town. He was hitchhiking and had no rhyme or reason as to why he chose to stop in this particular town, except that he was tired and it looked like a nice place to hang around in for a little while. Frankie's reply was the key to the next events that took place.

Gentry asked Frankie, "How would you like to become a full-fledged member of an association called, 'The Pythons?' Most people call us a gang. We like to think of ourselves as an organization."

Frankie answered, "I'm not sure I want to be a member. I'd like to think it over." The Governor had asked him to become a member as soon as he possibly could but something stopped Frankie from accepting their offer. He just couldn't go through with saying yes to these people.

Gentry said, "It's this simple. If you're not with us, you're against us. We don't tolerate outsiders in our territory. You don't have to be a member of the Pythons if you choose not to. However, there's one thing we forgot to tell you. If you decide not to accept our offer, you become nothing more than a flyspeck on a wall."

Frankie looked around the room and noticed that everyone seemed to have taken on a hypnotic glazed look he hadn't observed when they first arrived.

Frankie asked Gentry, "Are you threatening me?"

Gentry answered, "No, not at all. I don't threaten people. I'm simply stating facts."

Frankie replied, "I'm the new kid on the block. I simply can't allow you to force me to become a member of you're organization when I don't even know what it is."

Gentry replied, "No, we can't influence you to become part of our association. But we can throw you in the dungeon below. You can join the brave Hollywood hero, Rayven Delano."

Unexpectedly, several men grabbed Frankie and they put handcuffs on him. Frankie could have blown them all away with the blink of his eyes, but he wanted to see what was down under the building. When the time was right. He 'd rescue the movie star the Pythons had evidently kidnapped after all.

They put a blindfold on Frankie. He acted as though he couldn't see through the dark piece of cloth. Frankie simply went along with their miscalculated blunder to hold him, the powerful force fighter captive. Two men pushed him on the elevator and they started to descend downward. He concluded that the elevator stopped way below what would have been considered basement level.

Through his super x-ray vision Frankie observed the sharp contrast between the rooms upstairs and the dark, rough looking area they were taking him to. One of the rooms resembled a laboratory. Other areas were filled with enough weapons to declare war on the world. Another room contained hazardous bomb material, guns, knives, swords and grenades.

After passing by the rooms filled with weapons, they came to an area that looked like a medieval dungeon. There were deep crevices and several cave like entrances. Then, they came to an area where there were damp, dark jail cells with iron bars. The Pythons didn't take the handcuffs or the blindfold off Frankie until they had locked him in one of the cells directly next to the movie star.

The movie star, Rayven Delano, was swearing and demanding that the men let him out. The gang members laughed and went back upstairs on the elevator.

Rayven ranted and raved until the men were out of sight. He quieted down after a while, and then he asked Frankie how he happened to fall into the clutches of the Pythons?

Frankie said, "I guess it's because I came into their territory. They found me a place to live and gave me a job. After all the good fortune they handed me, they asked if I'd become one of them. I refused and several of them grabbed me. They handcuffed, blindfolded, and brought me down the elevator to this cell. What possible reason did they have for kidnapping you, Rayven?"

Rayven said, "I have no idea. It wasn't for ransom money. The Pythons don't need money. They're all richer than I am.

"The entire time they were dragging me to this cell they kept saying they were going to show the elected officials and Hollywood Mongols that they can't continue to influence the world! They continually repeated how much power the Pythons have on their side.

"The messages they relayed over and over were gibberish. I wasn't caught up in hobnobbing with politicians. Nor did I pay attention or have anything to do with world affairs. Why they wanted to kidnap me is a mystery. Since I've been in this cell I've tried to figure out what they're doing in this god-forsaken dungeon. I'm certain that whatever it is, it's not a pretty sight. They have been conducting some sort of experiments on unsuspecting people they lure into their trap. I can't see what the Pythons are doing, but sometimes I can hear them.

"They sound like a bunch of witches chanting incantations or whatever it's called. At times, I could hear voices yelling, no, no, don't change me. Please don't change me! Minutes later, I'd hear something that sounded like an animal. Then, I heard the Pythons praising someone or something. They're always bragging among themselves as to which member has more power.

"One thing is for certain. This place is creepy and the Pythons are weirdoes, pretending to be do-gooders and law-abiding citizens. They bring me the newspaper every day. Simply to show off news articles about the enormous amount of money they donate to different charities or the many starving people they feed at the missions. Makes me want to throw up every single time they swagger down here and throw the paper in my cell, boasting about how much good they do for everyone."

While Frankie silently listened very carefully to everything Ravyen was telling him, he decided not to break out of the cell and rescue Rayven just yet. He needed to play it cool a while longer. He wanted to witness more of the gang's activities. Some of the witch tales Rayven told him were too much. He never gave much thought to the occult. Frankie thought witches and sorcerers were a figment of people's imaginations and make believe. The young force fighter never came across a witch in his crime fighting experiences. Nor had he ever dealt with anyone that tried to cast spells. Even the spirit men he'd seen didn't try anything spectacular. They just vanished into thin air.

Rayven and Frankie talked a few more hours. Then, they both fell asleep for a short while before the Pythons woke them up. Gene came down to the dungeon, singing, "Rise and shine beautiful people. I brought you poor slobs some breakfast." He held a tray laden with food, water and coffee. He stuck the food and drinks between the small openings in the bars of the cell.

Frankie said, "I don't understand why you want to keep us in a cell. Neither Rayven nor I are a threat to the gang. We only want to leave and go our own way."

Gene asked them, "Are you guys ready to become Python members?"

Rayven and Frankie both said, "No way!"

"Well then," Gentry remarked, "I'm afraid you gentlemen will have to stay in the dungeon until you're ready to concede. I can guarantee that if you were to cooperate, you would both be well treated and richer than you could ever hope to imagine."

Frankie said, "I'd rather be dirt poor and live in this stinking cell the rest of my life then become a member of the Pythons."

Gene said, "Gentleman, your wish just might come true. You might live here forever. The word forever doesn't necessarily mean you have a long time to enjoy our hospitality. Especially since you don't have a family that would bother to look for you, and no one seems to care about Mr. has been movie actor Rayven Delano. No one has even bothered to report that he is missing."

Frankie said, "Surely you must know you can't get away with holding us hostage. If anything happens to either one of us, all the members of your organization will be held responsible and accountable."

Gene said, "You don't get it. No one gives a darn about the two of you insignificant individuals. You could disappear off the face of the earth. Who's to say you were ever born to begin with?" With those famous last words, Gene strutted back to the elevators and went upstairs. Little did Gene know that Frankie could break the bars on the cell door in a flash and with a certain look of his star eyes he could put Gene out of commission.

Frankie wanted to see what else was in the dungeon. He wasn't ready to reveal who he was just yet. The only way he could investigate further was to put Rayven to sleep while he explored. He figured the Python gang must have an overall plan to their madness.

With one quick glance, Frankie put Rayven to sleep. Next, he opened his cell door and headed toward the cave like entrance he noticed earlier. He strolled into the entrance leading to the rounded cave openings. The cave was dark and smelled rank and damp. He flashed his powerful eyes and lit up the cave so he could see where he was going. There were candles placed on small circular tables. There were jars of different kinds of roots and herbs neatly lined up on the shelves along the walls. Further down was another opening with a sealed door. Frankie thought he'd better employ safety first and utilize his ability to see through the door instead of blindly walking into a trap. Inside the room was the strangest sight. The dingy room was filthy. There were animals that looked part human. They were making weird moaning noises and fighting with one another over a morsel of food lying in a filthy dirt heap in the middle of the room. Frankie couldn't imagine what the heck the sight represented. It was excruciatingly painful to see the magnitude of evil behind the freakish beings behind the heavy metal door.

Walking back out of the cave the force fighter's mind was swirling ninety miles an hour. Good golly miss molly! What are those things?

What are the Pythons doing with the mutants? How could a medieval place like this still exist in this day and age? The cave must have been hidden underground for eons. The Pythons might have uncovered it when they remodeled the building.

Just then, Frankie heard a noise and instantly transported himself back inside the cell. Then he woke Rayven up.

The elevator doors clanged open. A man walked toward them with another tray of food and drinks. He was a small, mousy looking character that introduced himself as Jim. He asked Frankie and Rayven if they needed anything.

Jim seemed different than the other members so Frankie seized the opportunity to talk to him.

"Yes. We do need something," Frankie replied.

Jim asked, "What do you need? If I can, I'll try to bring it down to you."

Frankie said, "We need is to get out of here. Can you help us?"

"I feel sorry for you, Frankie and Rayven. But that is the one thing I can't do. I don't want to get in trouble with the other Pythons," Jim replied.

Rayven asked, "What possible reason could you have for wanting to become one of the gang?"

Jim exclaimed, "I didn't have a dime to my name and no one to turn to. They took me off the streets and gave me a job, money, and a place to live. I feel fortunate to be one of them. Even though I don't like all the things the Pythons do, on the whole, they are good people. I'm not going to cross them.

Frankie remarked, "If, they are such good folks, why did they kidnap me and Rayven, then lock us up and threaten our lives if we don't join their group? We didn't do anything to cross them. Rayven and I just didn't want to be a part of their organization. That doesn't give them cause to throw us in a dark, damp dungeon until they wear down our resistance and we agree to become a gang member."

Jim said, "I can bring you something to eat, drink, or read. I can't help you escape. I'm not allowed to be down here more than a few minutes." With that, Jim turned around and scurried back to the elevator.

Rayven said, "Frankie, what are we going to do now? I can't take one more day in this smelly cell without cracking up. I don't see anyway out of here. Even if we could get out of these foul cells, the only way out of here is on the elevator. They would grab us the second we arrived on the upper floor."

Frankie said, "Rayven, don't worry anymore. We are going to get out of here. But not before we find out what that malicious gang is up to.

Rayven asked, "How do you propose to accomplish that?"

Frankie said, " Here's what we will do. The next time they come back, let's agree to become members just long enough to see what there up to. That way we can gain access to the upstairs floor again. We'll know in our heart that we haven't conceded. The longer we resist, the longer they will hold us captive. I give you my word, Rayven. I won't let them harm a hair on your head."

Rayven said, "Oh yes Frankie, you and whose army is going to protect us from all the people that belong to this freaky gang?"

Frankie reassured Rayven when he said, "Trust me. It will be okay, just follow my lead."

" All right," Rayven said, "Fighting for our life is better than rotting in this cell. I knew I couldn't do anything by myself. Maybe between the two of us we can come up with a plan." They talked a while longer before they heard the elevator door open again.

Gentry and Fred came down to their cell. They handed Frankie and Rayven some fresh water to drink. Gentry said, "Are both you boys ready to concede and join the gang?"

Frankie and Rayven's answer took Gentry by surprise. Frankie and Rayven both said, "Okay you convinced us. We've thought it over and we both agree to join the Pythons. We aren't happy about being forced to join your club but we decided it would be better to be a part of something than to be part of nothing in this miserable cell."

A big smile came over Gentry's face. He said, "Thats great. The first thing we need to do is fix you both up with a room where you can shower and put on some clean clothes."

Gentry turned to Fred and said, " Take Frankie and Rayven to one of the rooms down by the elevator and show them where everything they need to groom with is located.

Gene turned to Frankie, and Rayven and said, "No need to say how bad you both smell, is there?"

Rayven and Frankie both answered, "No sir, there is no need for that."

Fred unlocked the cell and took Frankie and Rayven to an enormous apartment near the elevator. The funny thing is, the further away they walked from the area where the barred cells and caves were, the nicer it got. Nothing smelled damp and rank. It was like walking into another world. There was lush beige carpeting on the floors in the apartment. There were two bathrooms with a tub and a shower, a kitchenette, and two bedrooms with a huge closet that was filled with clothes. Gentry and Fred sat down in an easy chair and made themselves comfortable. The two men waited until Frankie and Rayven were through grooming.

When Frankie and Rayven were ready, Gentry asked them to sit down. He went on to say, "I know you're both upset with the Pythons. You feel we're all criminals and con artists, but we are neither.

"Rayven, the reason we kidnapped you was because we were tired of the misconception surrounding all the movies you make portraying witches. You're always portraying witches as being ugly and evil, when in fact there are good witches that are not hideous and wicked. They are called, 'White Witches.'

Then Gentry turned his attention to Frankie and said, "Frankie, we put you in a cell because we found out that you were a detective and you were spying on us. The Pythons wanted to teach both of you a lesson."

Frankie asked Gentry, "How did you know I was a detective?"

Gentry said, "When you didn't want to join the Pythons we assumed you were a spy because strangers don't often mosey around the area unless they're seeking the Pythons out to become one of us. We have people in high places on our payroll. It didn't take us long to find out what your true identity was."

Frankie inquired, "What are you implying when you say, 'become one of us?' Do you mean, members of your organization?"

Gentry replied, "No. I mean to actually become one of us. We are a part of the good white witches I told you about. We don't want to harm anyone. We merely want our own community to exist in without outsiders bothering us.

"We bought all the property in the area that I didn't inherit. We built this part of town up to show the rest of the community that we are civilized and just want to live and let live. We simply want the same things and the same rights everyone else has. Our members have families and children too."

Frankie asked, "How can you call yourself good witches? Isn't a witch just that, a witch? Is it true witches cast spells and do way out things using sorcery?"

Gentry exclaimed, "Witchcraft is our way of life. It's our religion. Due to all the misconceptions people use to judge us by, we simply want to govern among ourselves. We take care of our own in a manner that we see fit. We hold congregational meetings the outside community wouldn't understand. The lawmakers would accuse the members of our association for every crime that was ever committed in the vicinity. We take care of the bad witches ourselves, in our own way."

Frankie inquired, "If you're a witch, then who do you worship, who is your god?"

Gentry replied, "We worship our leader the same as other people worship whomever their god is."

Frankie responded, "That doesn't answer my question. Don't you know that worshipping a leader or a god should be from your own free will? You've been trying to force Rayven and myself to become a witch and worship your leader against our will. No matter what your motives are. Your gang kidnapped Rayven and I and locked us in a cell until we agreed to be a part of the Pythons. Now what are you really saying?"

Gentry said, "If both of you will accept our way's and become one of us, neither of you will want anything more out of life than to please our leader. You'll be showered with as much money as you want. You could live any place you choose. We have witches all over the world. We don't need the law to tell us how to govern our coven. We take care of rebellious witches that commit crimes. We don't want them to call attention to us if they are caught."

Frankie said, "I'm curious. How do you take care of the so-called bad witches?"

"We change their entire being and lock them up in a special cell that they can never escape from," Gentry replied.

Frankie thought to him self, well that explains the mutants he saw locked up in one of the caves.

Gentry turned to Rayven and asked, "Do you have any question's you'd like to ask before we begin our meeting with the other members?"

Rayven replied, "I have more than a hundred questions. First of all, let me say that you had no right to kidnap and lock me in a smelly cell. The movies I act in are not for real. They are made up, make believe roles. I'm merely an actor playing a part. That doesn't mean every role I play is the way it is. I don't suppose you will tell us why the Pythons have an arsenal of weapons?"

Gentry said, "That's enough information! I'm not answering any more questions from either one of you. The other members will be down soon."

Just then there was a knock on the door. Gentry opened it. One of the members came in, dressed in a red robe with a gold sash wrapped around his waist. Naturally, that caught Frankie's attention because it was the same outfit he saw on some of the spirit beings. Before they left the room, Gentry and Fred put on the same red outfit. They all walked down a long hallway to another enormous room. It was filled with over a hundred other red robed men and women.

They all turned and chanted some drivel as Gentry entered the room. Gentry led Frankie and Rayven to the front of the room. There were benches placed close to a podium. The only light in the room came from the candles. Gentry beckoned Frankie and Rayven to sit down on one of the benches. Fred and Gene sat on either side of them.

Gentry greeted everyone in the room. Then he introduced Frankie and Rayven. The meeting began. Of all things, the Python members started to sing a song much like the hymn's one would sing in church. However, the words in the songs they were singing were garbled and made no sense to Rayven and Frankie. The witches held a wand in their hand. They waved them in the air as they danced around the room. The group made animal sounds while chanting and throwing smelly herbs everywhere. After the disgusting display, they all sat down again.

Gentry went back to the podium and started the meeting. He called on Jim to read the minutes of the last meeting. Jim didn't say anything earth shattering. He read about a family that moved to another city and a family that had a new baby. There was an announcement of an upcoming marriage. They talked about the success of a potluck dinner they held the other night for several witches from another country that had been visiting with some of the Python members.

Jim sat back down. Gentry asked the other members if there was any new business? One of the members talked about buying a building and opening up another restaurant. Another stood and asked if his family could be transferred to a foreign country. It was boring stuff and it seemed to go on forever.

Things began to perk up when one of the members asked if they could vote on hiring a foreign doctor that applied for a new position that was opening up in the laboratory. They all said aye and the foreigner was hired. After they voted on the doctor, Gentry said, "As you know, we don't allow an outsider to attend a meeting unless they go through the ritual. Let's see a show of hands on how many members would like to initiate Frankie and Rayven?" Every hand in the place went high in the air. Gentry motioned Frankie and Rayven to stand in front of the podium, and then he said, "Let the games begin."

All the members stood up. A few of them started to play a small wooden drum and flutes. Some of them wove around, chanting and making weird animal noises. They took Frankie and Rayven and strapped them to a chair in the middle of the room. They gathered around Frankie and Rayven in a circle. One of the members came in through a door that led to the laboratory. He was holding a leash attached to an animal that looked to be part human. It had the face of a human with a bushy lion's main all around it's head. It's ears looked like pig ears that were sewn on. The rest of his body looked like a lion, struggling to walk upright.

Rayven asked, "What on God's green earth is that?"

Frankie replied, "I don't know. Whatever you do, don't act afraid."

Rayven said, "Are you kidding? I'm petrified."

The beast wasn't one of the mutants Frankie had seen in the cave. The weird looking being came up to Frankie and Rayven. He stood right in front of them making funny sounds, acting as if it was going to harm them.

Frankie merely looked into the half human, half animal's eyes and the beast couldn't move. Frankie was silently communicating with it. The beast mentally told Frankie he was human. He didn't want to be a witch. When he tried to leave the doctors experimented on him. The human animal beast silently conveyed that he didn't want to harm them. The witches were forcing him to scare them into joining the group.

A few witches picked up on the way the human like animal and Frankie were looking at one another and silently communicating. One of the witches waved a wand at the beast and it fell to the ground. Frankie had witnessed enough. Witches acting like they were simply good old boys, and the pillars of the community that take the law into their own hands. Forcing people to become a witch, kidnapping Rayven, and Frankie, experimenting on humans and animals, building an arsenal, and endorsing evil wicked beings in the cave that were groveling in filth. Frankie had witnessed enough to know these people could act like they were well brought up do gooders. They were indeed, calloused, and wicked.

To the witches bewildering amazement, Frankie broke the straps that were binding him and he stood up. With one look and a sweep of his hand in the air, steel chains came flying down from the ceiling in every direction. Everyone in the room, except for Rayven and the beast, were chained to one another and to the steel hooks Frankie had zapped down from the ceiling. Frankie freed the awestruck Rayven and told him not to worry. Then, he touched the wretched animal looking man lying on the floor. Instantly, the beast turned back into a handsome blond haired, blue-eyed human being, sobbing his heart out as Frankie comforted him. The securely bound witches started cursing spells at Frankie. He simply waved his hand and sealed their mouths shut so they couldn't speak another word.

Rayven asked Frankie, "Are you an angel?"

Frankie said, "No Rayven. I'm just a man fulfilling a destiny to fight crime and evil. Outside of my two brothers and Sam, this is the first time anyone else has been privy to witness my powers to fight evil forces."

Frankie took the blond man named Robert and Rayven by the hand and led them to the elevator. Frankie told them they were free to go. Needless to say, Robert and Rayven didn't want to leave Frankie's side. They wanted to stay with Frankie and wait for the police to pick up the Python gang. They wanted to tell the police to lock the witches up and throw away the key.

Frankie said, "The Python gang won't get away with kidnapping charges or for the cache of weapons they have stashed in the building. I'm sure the authorities will find enough evidence to link those criminals to some of the unsolved mysteries, including Senator Gray's misfortune."

Without anyone being aware of his actions, the second after he bound the so called good witches in chains, with the blink of his eye, Frankie disintegrated every distorted mutant evil thing that he'd seen behind the steel doors within the dark, damp cave. He sealed the cave off so the police wouldn't see it had even existed. Although the Pythons were still citizens and had the right to due process, Frankie was going to make sure that the gang members were locked up in a prison cell for quite a spell.

Frankie, Rayven, and Robert went outside to clear their head in the fresh air. Rayven said, "Whoopee! It sure feels good to breathe fresh air again. Let's stand out here and wait for the police."

They all breathed a sigh of relief when they heard the sirens coming around the corner. As soon as the police cars pulled up in front of the building Frankie, Robert, and Rayven, immediately asked if one of the officers would give them a ride. They wanted to get out of the witch-infested area as fast as the squad car could drive them. They asked the officer to drive them to the finest hotel in town but to make sure it was clear on the other side of town.

When they reached the hotel Frankie said, "Rayven, would you register a room for me too? I'll be right back." The force fighter zipped back to the Natas building to make sure the officers were getting the job done without any trouble. He wanted to flatten the building right then and there and destroy the evil that took place within the confines of the structure. He knew he couldn't raze the building until the police were done and everyone was out of the building. The officers would no doubt be casing the place the rest of the evening to see if there were any other rooms filled with weapons and paraphernalia that could have led to mass destruction.

There was nothing more Frankie could accomplish tonight so he zoomed back to the hotel. Before calling it a night he asked Rayven and Robert if they would like to go with him to the restaurant in the hotel and grab a cup of coffee and something to eat. Robert and Rayven shook their heads in agreement. After they placed their order, quite naturally, the first topic of conversation on the events of the night was Frankie's astronomical deeds.

Rayven said, "Frankie, I never thought we'd see daylight again. I had no idea I was in a cell next to a man with the powers of a super hero."

Frankie said, "Rayven, I'm not a super hero. I'm a force fighter. I've been appointed to right some of the wrongs when I'm faced with them. My being here was no accident. Someone greater than me guides my fate and endowed me with awesome capabilities of power to fight villainous behavior."

Robert asked, "How did you simply touch me and restore my face and body to be exactly the way it was before the witches butchered me?"

Frankie said, "Robert, the same force that gave me the power to fight evil, simply touched you through me. I want you to remember this one fact. My good man, you helped heal yourself because there was no evil in your heart. You were a victim. If there had been any wicked way within your heart, you would still look like you did before I touched you."

Rayven said, "Robert, how did you happen to get mixed up with the Pythons?"

Robert said, "Gentry and I had been friends since grade school. For a while we went our own way. Six months ago I moved back to town. I looked Gentry up and we struck up our old friendship. I had no idea Gentry was practicing occult rituals. It wasn't long before Gentry approached me to become one of them. I refused at first. Then, later on just to get him off my back, I agreed to join. I didn't know what I was letting my self in for. Once I saw the ceremonies the witches performed, I didn't want any part of them. Needless to say, they wouldn't let me leave. You both saw what they did to me when I wouldn't participate."

"Robert, did you happen to know if the Pythons knew Senator Gray?" Frankie asked.

Robert said, "Yes. Senator Gray was a witch too. He was starting to back off and make waves so they got rid of him."

Frankie thought, well what do you know! Governor Rick was right after all.

Robert and Rayven both said, "Frankie, we want to stay right by you're side all the time for the rest of our lives."

Frankie said, "There's nothing I'd like more than to have you with me, but that's impossible. I'd like us to keep in touch with one another and we could get together whenever it's possible. If you ever need anything, money, a job, or a place to stay, you can look me up anytime.

Frankie said, "Rayven, and Robert, I know it is unrealistic to think I can fight crime without ever giving myself away from time to time. I need to take you both into my confidence. I'm asking both of you to keep everything I did when I apprehended the witches a secret. I know my actions must have seemed improbable. I can't go into any further details concerning the destiny that has been set forth for me. All I can say is that it comes from a force more powerful than mine. I have to leave it at that. I must remain as anonymous and low-keyed as I possibly can. I'm sure IAM knows why you were both allowed to witness my powers. Don't volunteer any information as to what actually took place in the dungeon. I'll take care of giving the police and the governor the details. Let them come to their own conclusions about the manner in which the witches were apprehended.

Rayven and Robert both said, "Of course, Frankie. We promise never to reveal anything that took place tonight. We will do whatever we can to keep your secret. What do we say to the officials when we're asked about the super phenomenon that happened tonight?"

Frankie requested that Rayven and Robert could simply say, "It all happened to fast, all they knew for certain was that one-minute they were both held captive and the next they were rescued."

Robert and Rayven were so enthralled with Frankie they agreed to do whatever they could to help. After they had their fill of pie and coffee they left the restaurant, bid each other good night and went to their rooms.

Bright and early the next morning, Frankie left a note on Rayven and Robert's hotel door explaining that he didn't have time to meet them for breakfast. He wrote his address and phone number on the note and told them to contact him anytime they wanted to. Frankie wished them both the best of luck. He left the hotel and drove a rented car over to the Natas building.

Frankie scanned inside the structure to make sure no one was inside. When he saw it was all clear, the first thing he did was to destroy the entire dungeon area by reducing it to smithereens. He was going to make certain no one ever had access to the medieval place again. Then with a look, he razed the building to a heap of rubble. When everyone in the area heard the noise they ran out doors to see what was going on. Frankie couldn't stand the thought of the building being used for anything after all the wicked things he witnessed in it.

He thought the city could just wonder what happened to the structure without his input. Mission complete. Frankie got in his car and drove straight home without making one stop along the way.

When he arrived home Cynthia was waiting to greet him. She said, "Frankie, you've been gone so long. I missed you so much."

Frankie remarked, "I'm home now. I hope I don't have to go anywhere for very long time. How is my family doing? We're they worried about me?"

Cynthia said, "Your family is fine. Naturally they're concerned. You were gone longer than you said you would be."

Frankie replied, "I was working undercover and I couldn't telephone anyone. I'm exhausted. I don't feel much like talking right now. I need to freshen up and catch some sleep. If you need me, I'll be resting at my grandparent's house for the rest of the day."

When Frankie walked into his grandparent's house he thought of how wonderful it felt to be in familiar surroundings where the first thing you're aware of is the aroma of fresh baked bread and cookies. It was so good to be home. He loved being in the clean fresh sweetness with people he loved. Grandma and Grandpa greeted Frankie and asked him to sit and eat some of the warm goodies.

Frankie said, "You don't have to twist my arm. These are the best cookies you ever made Grandma. Do you mind if I freshen up and sleep here a while?"

Grandma said, "Grandson, you know you're always welcome to stay. The spare room upstairs is ready and waiting."

Frankie said, "Thanks I'm exhausted. I think I'll take a shower and hit the hay. Good night Grandma and Grandpa. Or I should say good morning. Frankie went upstairs, took a quick shower, and fell fast asleep.

CHAPTER 13...
HOME SWEET HOME

Frankie woke up to the sound of laughter coming from downstairs. He got dressed and ran down the stairs to greet Joe and Greg. They both said, "Hello younger brother. We missed your smiling face. How have you been?"

Frankie said, "I'm fine. "What's been going on with the two of you?"

Joe said, "Nothing much. We've just been keeping the home fires burning while you've been away. We stopped by to see how you were and to ask if you needed anything?"

Frankie replied, "No thanks. I was just resting."

Joe asked, "Would you like to have supper with both you're brothers this evening?"

Frankie said, "Okay. Pick me up around six o'clock. I'm still kind of tired so I'm going to go back to sleep a while longer."

Grandpa sensed something wasn't quite right with Frankie's demeanor. So he asked Frankie to sit down with him for a while. Grandpa quietly asked Frankie, "What's bothering you son?"

"Nothing much." Frankie said.

Gramps said, "I'm not so old that I can't tell when you're troubled."

Frankie said, "All right Granddad, I'll tell you. I'm not sure it's going to make much sense. When I'm fighting crime I see so many things it makes me wonder why people have to be so wicked? Why do they want to harm one another? Why can't there be peace and harmony?"

Grandpa said, "Frankie boy, it's going to be that way until the Mighty One intervenes."

Mystified, Frankie asked, "Who is the Mighty One? Why doesn't he intervene before things grow steadily worse? I went to church and Sunday school and believe there is a God. Nevertheless, I wasn't taught about evil spirits lurking in every nook and cranny. I do question why God doesn't do something to stop the violence, the wars, and the turmoil now, instead of letting wickedness continue to escalate."

Grandpa said, "It might look like the Mighty One is not doing anything but that doesn't mean he isn't. He gave men the free will to live in peace in harmony but many people choose not to. There was a time when it was considered part of our history and heritage to pray every morning in school before the first class of the day started. Yet, I've heard there is a crusade-taking place to take prayer out of school because it's offensive to those who don't believe in God. It seems improbable in this day and age to think our great grandchildren won't be allowed to pray in school.

"No matter how much things change. My generation will remember the way we had the freedom to honor God in all things, whether it was in public or in the privacy in our homes. I'm beginning to think that the heart of man grows colder and colder with each passing day. So many people are doing their own thing, in their own way of anything goes. If it feels good, do it regardless of whom it harms or hurts. That's why I think crime and evil is on the rise. There are those who worship their strange gods or a cow or whatever or whomever they have made their god and I think that opens the door for more evil spirits to invade the earth.

"You see Frankie, not many people believe there is a spirit world fighting to destroy all of mankind. Many believe the devil isn't real. All that myth does is allow the spirits to become stronger. Some religions fear teaching about Satan or evil beings. As far as that goes, not everyone believes there is a God or that it was the Almighty that created mankind"

Frankie said, "Grandpa, I understand a little more than you think I do about the spirit world. What would you say if I told you I've seen evil in action?"

Grandpa remarked, "Frankie, I'm sure you can't help but see what certain people are capable of doing in the line of work that you're in. Out there fighting crime and seeing twisted behavior."

Frankie said. "No Grandpa. I mean I actually see the spirits. They are nothing like anything I've ever read or heard about. The leader is not the little red guy with a forked tail holding a pitchfork. He's not some ugly looking creature. On the contrary, the wicked spirits I've seen are handsome."

A look of surprise came over Grandpa's face. He said, "Frankie, I've always believed evil spirits were as ugly and grotesque as the wicked deeds they perform. Nevertheless, I've never heard you speak with such authority. I can hear in your voice that you've seen something. It's a special gift to be able to see into the spirit world."

Frankie said, "Gramps, you're right. But I don't feel special. I feel like I want to stomp the wicked beings into the ground. I've seen the damage and havoc they reek in their quest to destroy people."

Grandpa remarked. "I always believed evil spirits hated mankind. They are jealous God created man in God's image and breathed life from his very own mouth right into man's mouth.

"This has been an interesting conversation and one I never thought you and I would ever have. I've known about spirits for a good many years. I don't say much about it. I continue to pray a sheltering shield be placed around my loved ones. Praying is the only way to keep our family safe from wicked beings. I'm not going to give them a chance to invade our safe haven.

"Sorry grandson. I don't mean to preach. Do you realize that since the beginning of time there has been a fascination over good versus evil? The attraction has made some people a lot of money. Sometimes evil is simply referred to as bad or the devil made me do it. Books, movies, folklore and everything in everyday living are surrounded with things that point to whatever we do as being either good or bad. Even harmless western movies have the good guys and the bad guys. There's no place to hide from those facts of life. We simply do the best we can and try to be included as part of the good guys."

Frankie said, "Thank you, Granddad."

The young force fighter was still tired. He excused himself and went back upstairs to sleep awhile longer. While he was sleeping he dreamt about visiting the purple planet he seen floating ever so slowly in space. It was such a peaceful serene dream. Frankie didn't wake up until Joe came up to the bedroom and said, "Wake up sleepy head. Its suppertime."

Frankie got up. After he threw some water on his face and freshened up they both walked downstairs together. They said good-bye to Grandma and Grandpa and went on their merry way. On route to the restaurant, Joe told Frankie that Greg was going to meet them there.

They arrived at their destination, parked the car, and started walking toward the restaurant. Out of the blue, Frankie said, "Joe, would you like to go with me to visit a new planet?"

Joe remarked, "I'm not sure I want to go. I had a great time when you took me flying through outer space. I loved Planet Moonazer. Nevertheless, I like my feet planted firmly on the ground. Maybe Greg would like to go?"

Frankie said, "All right. I'll ask Greg later."

The boys always enjoyed one another's company. They laughed and talked throughout the meal. After they were done eating Frankie said, "I'm going to have you drop me off at Cynthia's.

Out of the blue, Joe said, "I've been dating Kathleen."

"So are you sweet on Kathleen?" Frankie asked.

Joe said, "At first, I just wanted to spend some time with Kathleen because I felt sorry for her. She was having such a rough time. Each time I was with her I got to know her a little better. I think she is really sweet. She's been helping with a few of the younger girls living in the TLC home. Yes, I guess I'd have to say, I'm kind of sweet on Kathleen."

Frankie asked, "What about you Greg? Who are you sweet on?"

Greg became quiet and looked like he was off in space. Then he said, "No one special." He didn't tell his brothers he couldn't stop thinking about Melinda on planet Moonazer.

Joe and Frankie both kidded around with Greg a little while longer then decided it was time to go about their business. As they were leaving the restaurant Greg said, "I have some work to finish up so I'll see you guys tomorrow.

Joe and Frankie said, "All right. See you later."

Joe drove Frankie to Cynthia's house and dropped him off.

Frankie was deep in thought as he walked up the few stairs to Cynthia's front porch. He was about to knock when the door opened. Cynthia stood in the doorway smiling. He thought she looked just like an angel. He stood there staring at her and all of a sudden, the weight of the world he seemed to be carrying on his shoulders disappeared. Frankie thought Cynthia looked more beautiful than ever. He took in her tiny figure with the long dark hair flowing down her back. Her beautiful green eyes were shining brightly under the glare of the porch light.

Frankie said, "Come out here Cynthia. I want to ask you something. In a serious, quiet voice, he said, "Cynthia, I love you."

She looked at him very seriously, and then, she said, "What brought that on?"

Smiling sheepishly, Frankie merely stared at her.

With her eyes still sparkling Cynthia looked absolutely radiant when she said, "I love you too, Frankie. I've known since I was five years old that you were the only one for me."

Frankie said, "Wait here a minute. I have to run home and get something."

Five minutes later, Frankie was standing in her front yard with his guitar, singing a love song. When he finished singing he walked up to where she was sitting on the porch swing, got on his knees, and said, "Cynthia, will you marry me?"

She was so touched by his romantic overture. Her heart was pounding and her cheeks were flushed as tears of happiness started to flood her eyes.

Cynthia said, "Oh yes, yes, yes, Frankie, I will marry you."

Although Cynthia knew that someday they would be married, she never expected anything so wonderfully romantic to happen when Frankie finally popped the question. The marriage proposal was the most thrilling experience of her life.

Just about that time, her parents opened the screen door to see what was going on. Cynthia excitedly blurted out the news, "Mom, Dad, Frankie and I are going to be married."

Her parents practically danced over to both of them. They were laughing, and hugging, and congratulating them all at the same time. Mr. Butler asked, Frankie, do you're parents know about the happy news?"

Frankie said, "No. My parents don't know yet. I just got the bright idea to ask Cynthia to marry me the instant I seen her standing in the doorway. I love your daughter. I don't want to wait any longer. She is the only woman I will ever want to be with for the rest of my life. We were going to wait until I was through with college. I just decided there is no reason I can't have my woman and get an education at the same time. We set the date for two months from today so it doesn't give us much time to make the arrangements. What do you say Mr. & Mrs. Butler, should we go across the street to my parent's and tell them the happy news together?"

Arm in arm, Mr. & Mrs. Butler and Cynthia walked across the street giggling and dancing while Frankie strummed his guitar and sang."

Mom and Dad Stargazer heard Frankie serenading Cynthia. They were already sitting outside on the porch swing watching the scene that was taking place at their neighbor's house.

Frankie said, "Guess what happened folks?"

Mom said, "I'm not sure. If I have to guess, I'd say maybe you're trying to wake up the whole neighborhood. Just like the time you and Sam did when you decided to hold a concert on the sidewalk at one o clock in the morning. I'll never forget that. I'm sure the neighbors won't ever forget that antic either. A few neighbors probably heard the concert you we're performing in the Butler's front yard and they chalked it up to one of the Stargazer boys acting up again."

Frankie said, "Mom, If you're through embarrassing me now, I'd like to tell you and Dad that Cynthia and I are getting married in two months."

Mom said, " Oh, son, I'm sorry I teased you." Both Mom and Dad jumped off the porch swing at the same time. They congratulated Cynthia and Frankie and held both of them in their arms. Then the Butler's and the Stargazer's were all hugging at once.

Dad and Mom Stargazer finally got their composure back. Dad said, "We watched both of you children grow up together for a good many years. We know the way you both feel about one another. Nevertheless, we still weren't expecting a wedding to take place this soon."

Mr. & Mrs. Stargazer told Cynthia how very happy they were that she was going to officially be part of the family, even though she has always been like one of their own children. After the congratulations and jubilant laughter, both their parents went into the house and left Frankie and Cynthia alone.

Cynthia asked Frankie, "What made you ask me to marry you tonight of all nights? I thought you wanted to wait until you got a law degree?"

Frankie said, "Cynthia, my job takes me out of town so much of the time. When I'm out of town all I do is I think about you. I miss you the entire time I'm away.

"Tonight, when I saw you standing in the doorway looking sweet and pretty, it dawned on me. There was no reason we shouldn't be together now. I like the thought of having you by my side all the time. I've often envisioned you waiting for me to come home and throwing your arms around me the second I walk in the door. I'm earning enough money to take care of you. We both knew we wanted to marry some day and that day is here and now.

"I'm sorry I didn't have a ring to put on your finger tonight when I asked you to marry me. I'm going to get you one that will knock your eyes out and make the other girls pea green with envy."

Cynthia said," Frankie, just a small inexpensive ring will be okay."

Frankie said, "Dear heart, have patience. I know exactly the kind of ring I want to put on your finger. It may take me a few days to locate the precise ring I wish to give to the girl of my dreams."

CHAPTER 14 ... EVIL REARS ITS UGLY FACE

Frankie wanted to take a trip to planet Moonazer to ask his friend, Matthew, if he would make him an engagement ring with some of the stones he saw on the planet. Matilda showed Frankie a ring Matthew made her when they were courting. Frankie decided right then and there that it was the same kind of ring he'd like to give to Cynthia some day.

He called his brother, Greg, and asked him if he wanted to go for a ride. Greg knew exactly what his brother meant. He jumped at the chance to go to Moonazer again.

Greg said, "When do you want to cruise?"

"Is tonight to soon?" Frankie asked.

Greg replied, "Heck no. It isn't soon enough."

Frankie laughed and said, "I have a few things to do before we leave. I'll come by your place sometime tonight.

The day flew by. Early that evening, just about the time the sun was starting to set, Frankie went over to pick up Greg. Once again they were on their way to play in outer space. It wasn't long before they were standing on Moonazer. Greg was ecstatic. He couldn't wait to see Melinda again. Matthew was standing by the fence smiling, ready to greet the boys in the warmest manner.

As they headed toward the house, Greg spotted Melinda in the garden. She spotted them coming down the walkway and scooted inside the house.

In the meantime, Matthew, Greg and Frankie walked down the flowered pathway that led to Matthew's residence. They walked in the back door and made themselves comfortable on the sofa. As

Matthew and Frankie talked on and on, one couldn't help notice there were sparks flying between Greg and Melinda the moment she walked into the room. Their countenance made the room appear brighter than it already was. When Frankie seen the way Melinda and Greg looked at each other he realized Melinda was the girl that Greg was in love with. Frankie knew there was no way the two of them could ever be together. He hoped Greg wasn't going to be hurt by his infatuation with Melinda.

Matthew asked, "What's new with the Stargazers and how is Sam doing? I really got a kick out of Sam's enthusiasm to invent a space machine that would take him wherever he wanted to go in the vastness of the Universe. Sam told me he wanted to dance around the stars to the rhythm of Mozart and Beethoven's music."

Frankie updated Matthew on Joe and Sam. Then he informed his friend of his recent engagement to marry Cynthia.

Matthew said, "Congratulation's Frankie. I'm pleased you've found the love of a woman, not just to keep you warm, but also to keep you in line."

Everyone in the room knew Matthew was teasing and they laughed heartily.

Frankie said, "Matthew, I came here to ask if you'd do something for me."

Matthew said, "Your wish is my command. What can I do for you?"

Frankie replied, " I admired the ring you made for Matilda. I told myself if I ever got brave enough to ask Cynthia to marry me, I'd ask if you'd make me an engagement ring. I kind of jumped the gun and asked my girlfriend to marry me and I didn't have a ring to put on her finger. Is it possible to make me a ring with the same beautiful blue and pink diamonds? I'll pay whatever you ask."

Matthew spoke. "I'm deeply honored you want to give the same kind of ring to the woman you love, that I gave to the woman I love. Wait here Frankie. I won't be gone long."

Matthew went outside into a small building that was located in the back yard beyond the flower garden.

Matilda said, "Frankie, I had no idea the craftsmanship of my ring made such an impression on you."

Frankie replied, "Ever since I saw your engagement ring, I knew right then and there it was the most beautiful ring I'd ever seen. I got the idea to have one made for Cynthia after you told me Matthew liked creating unique pieces of jewelry. I want to give Cynthia the best of everything."

Matilda and Frankie chatted awhile longer. Neither of them noticed when Melinda and Greg slipped out of the house. Frankie happened to glance out the window and spotted them sitting on a bench near the fishpond. They were laughing and talking as the tiny animals that lived in the garden flitted around their feet. He thought what a great painting the scene with Greg, Melinda and the animals would make. To bad Sam wasn't there to sketch it.

About that time, Matthew came in the house carrying a tiny ring box. Frankie was flabbergasted when he opened the ring box and saw what Matthew had designed in such a short time. The ring was fashioned in a different pattern than Matilda's ring but it was fabulous. It had a white Lindsey star set in a blue diamond. There were tiny pink and rainbow colored diamonds arranged in a circle around the blue diamond. The ring band looked as if it was made with a clear liquid gold that looked like glass. You could see right through it. Matthew even made similar matching wedding rings for both Cynthia and Frankie.

Through tear stained eyes, Frankie said, "The rings are beautiful and much more than I'd hoped for. How can I ever thank you or repay you for the most stunning rings in the world or I should say in the Universe. They are gorgeous and unlike anything on earth."

Matthew remarked, "You don't owe me anything. I was happy to be a small part of the most special event in your life."

Frankie said, "It takes a truly talented artist to fashion a design as breathtaking as these rings. I'll always treasure them. I'm sure Cynthia is going to be bowled over when she sees them. Frankie put the rings back in the ring box and slipped the box in his pocket.

Then, Frankie said, "Matthew, I wish you and your family could come to my wedding."

Matthew said, "You know that's impossible. Even though we can't attend your wedding ceremony I want you to know, we will be there in spirit."

Frankie replied, "Thank you Matthew. From the bottom of my heart, I thank you dear friend. I hope you won't think of me as being ungrateful but it's time to fetch Greg and head for home. Before I leave, I was wondering if is there anything at all that you can tell me about a purple planet I saw on the way to Moonazer?"

Matthew remarked, "That is a very special planet the 'Founding Father' created for different animals he formed throughout the ages.

Frankie asked, "Do you think it would be safe for Greg and me to visit the purple planet on the way home?

Matthew said, "Sure, you can stop and visit the purple planet. It's as safe as Moonazer and just as beautiful. It's patterned with different colors and different scenery."

Matthew, Matilda and Frankie walked over to the area where Greg and Melinda were sitting. They noticed the intense way Melinda and Greg were looking at one another. For just an instant, there appeared to be a look of concern on Matthew and Matilda's face.

Greg said, "I hope it was okay to come out to the garden and sit with your daughter. She was teaching me the customs and lifestyles of the people that live here."

Matilda replied. "We don't mind the two of you young people talking and getting to know the customs of the different worlds your both from. We are glad you could come to visit us, Greg. You're welcome anytime."

They bid one another farewell, and then, Frankie and Greg were on their way. Frankie told Greg on the route home he was going to make one more stop. He flew to the purple planet and they landed in the midst of it. The sky was white with different shades of violet. There was a golden cast to it. There were three purple moons casting shadows in the treetops. The colors of the landscape were sprinkled with diverse shades of green, brown, purple, gold, and blue.

The scenery was spectacular in a distinctively different fashion than the beauty on planet Moonazer. There were many different kinds of animals roaming around as far as the eye could see. The boys couldn't get over the fact that they were all as tame as they could be. They came right up to Greg and Frankie. At first, Greg was leery of the animals. When he saw how friendly they were, he warmed right up to them. Of course, the moment they landed, Frankie had no fear of the animals.

The weird and wonderful thing about the animals is the way the lion's were laying side by side with the lambs. It didn't matter what breed of animal it was, they were all friendly with one another. The lions were actually eating grass and leaves.

Frankie said, "I never heard of a lion eating grass and leaves before."

There were plants and vegetables growing on every inch of land. Greg and Frankie were not familiar with most of the plants and vegetables. They recognized carrots, beans, corn and peas among the different plants. They both thought it was strange that all the animals appeared to be vegetarians.

After they walked a little further down the field, the two brothers came across a cottage in the middle of the vast vegetable garden. The cottage was structured with tiny gold, green and white pebbles and the woodwork was trimmed in different shades of gold. There was a woman sitting on the porch petting several dogs and cats. When the woman glanced up and saw the boys walking toward her she stood up and waved her hand high in the air.

She called out, "Hey fellas! What are you doing so far away from home?"

Greg remarked, "Do you know where we live?"

The woman said, "Sure I do. You're from the Planet Earth."

Frankie asked, "How do you know we're from Earth?"

She replied, "I know by the way you look and the way you're dressed. I've seen pictures of earthlings in a book. This isn't a primitive planet in any sense of the word simply because there are animals roaming freely."

"What planet is this?" Frankie asked.

The woman said, "You're on 'Planet Purpling.'" How do you like it so far?"

They both replied that it was interesting and asked where did all the animals come from?

She said, "The animals came from everywhere. Don't you recognize them?"

They both said, "We recognize some of them but were not familiar with most of the animals that are roaming around."

Greg asked, "Do many people live on Planet Purpling?"

She said, "Yes. There are many people that live here. We are called animal caretakers, even though the animals take care of themselves. The food grows everywhere on the entire planet and replenishes itself. The minute one plant is eaten another pops up."

Greg replied, "I'm curious. With all these animals, how could it be that there were no animal droppings anywhere? The animals smell so fresh and they're all so clean."

She said, "Anything that is considered unclean is immediately sucked under the ground. The planet is equipped to take care of everything the animals require for their well-being. Not one animal ever preys upon the other and none of them eat meat.

"The planet was made to harbor and cater to animals from every part of the Universe. When animals die, their souls come to Planet Purpling and they receive another body. It's not the same as the one they had before death. They don't have to eat, unless they want to. They don't have offspring and their new bodies don't function the way they did before they came here. The food they eat is disposed of in another manner unknown to me.

"The baby animals roaming around here were not born on Purpling. They died at an early age, and then they came here. The animals don't age any further in their new bodies. They remain young and healthy."

Greg asked, "Is this an animal Heaven?"

She said, "Maybe it is and maybe it isn't."

Greg said, "My name is Greg Stargazer and this is my brother Frankie."

The lady replied, "My name is Trinka Tuneri.

Frankie asked, Trinka, how long have you lived on Purpling?

Trinka said, "I was born on Purpling. I've lived here all my life with my husband and two children."

Frankie came right out and asked her, "Do you know where the Black Planet is located?"

She looked Frankie straight in the eye, and said, "No one knows the exact location except for the Founding Father. We aren't allowed to talk about the dark planet. You mustn't ask any more questions pertaining to the Black Planet."

Trinka changed the subject and started to explain, " Hey boys would you like to know that some of the plants and trees are different colors in other areas of the planet. In the evening the sky over the entire planet turns a dark golden color. The planets purple color as seen in space covers the whole planet to hide the fact there is life on Planet Purpling. It also acts as a shield of defense to prevent evil forces from penetrating their territory.

Once again, Frankie inquired, "Is it okay to ask if you've heard about evil beings?"

Trinka said, "We certainly have heard of them. Haven't you fellas from earth heard about them?"

Frankie said, "Yes, we are aware of the forces of evil trying to take over the Universe. Once I even tried to find the unmentionable planet."

She said, "Well, you can forget that Frankie Stargazer. You will never find it. The Founding Father hid the Black Planet where no one can find it."

A few minutes later Frankie said, "Trinka, visiting planet Purpling and meeting you has been a unique and wonderful experience but we have to leave now. Maybe we'll meet again someday."

Trinka said, "All right, Frankie and Greg. Thanks for visiting. Come back anytime. The animals love people."

Frankie and Greg waved good-bye. They took off and were soaring into outer space once again. They were close to earth when Frankie perceived several spirits flying right in front of them. They had on the same red suits with gold sashes. They acted as though they were not aware Frankie was flying right behind them, right on their tail.

The spirit men didn't intimidate Frankie. Bravely, he flew right next to them. In a really loud voice Frankie said, "Boo stinky creeps. I see you." The spirits continued to act as if nothing unusual was happening. They acted like they didn't know Frankie was flying right next to them. He decided to follow the spirits and see what they were up to. He glanced up to see if his gigantic eagle friend was overhead. Sure enough, the eagle was right above him, watching over Frankie's every move.

The spirits reached the earth and landed in a remote area in a forest near the mountains. They stood there and talked a few minutes. Then they started to walk on a path leading uphill. They stopped halfway up the mountain and moved a huge rock that covered an opening in the mountainside. Frankie could see other spirits standing in the opening.

Frankie wasn't sure why they acted as if they didn't see him when he was flying in space. He recalled IAM'S warning to be on guard. The evil spirit men can make people believe something is one way when it's really another. They are masters of dark deception. They will forever and always deceive, lie, steal, cheat, kill and destroy every man, woman and child they possibly can.

Frankie said, "Greg, I want you to wait right here in this very spot were standing. I'll be right back. I want to check something out on the mountain over there."

Greg said, "Okay Frankie. Just don't forget where you left me."

I promise I'll remember where you are. I'll rocket down to pick you up in a few minutes.

Quick as a bullet, he zapped himself up the mountainside. Frankie didn't make himself invisible. Instead, he hid behind a rock near the opening. One of the spirits spotted him and once more, the spirit disappeared instantly. Frankie thought the reason he couldn't focus in on their destination when they vanish into thin air was because the beings probably be-bopped back to the Black Planet.

Frankie wanted to find the dreaded Black Planet in the worst way and annihilate all of the evil beings at one time, so they couldn't tempt anyone ever again. He knew it wasn't going to be that simple. Possibly, his vigor to destroy the spirit men in his own way is the reason IAM kept the location a secret. As yet, IAM didn't instruct Frankie on the intricate details of the plan he has in store for the evil Spirits. Frankie knew he had to be patient and use wisdom until he knew the whole story and the methods IAM was going to teach him in his quest to battle and destroy the foul enemy.

Frankie whooshed back to the spot where he left Greg waiting. His brother wasn't there. He focused his eyes and scanned every inch of the entire area, but Greg was nowhere to be found. Frankie called out, "IAM, are you there? I'm stumped. I can't find my brother Greg?"

At once Frankie heard the sound of IAM'S voice booming in the treetops.

IAM said, "Fear not, for I am with you. The wicked spirit men were aware of your presence the entire time you were flying near them. They knew you landed in the forest. They tricked you into following their trail to the mountainside. Several of the evil spirit men lurk in the forest all the time. Tonight they made their appearance visible. They disguised themselves as fisherman and took Greg to one of their fortifications in the forest.

"Don't worry. They can't harm Greg. He has the light inside his heart and he belongs to the good spirit. The reason you couldn't find Greg is very simple. You're trying to scan the area with your eyes open. What you need to do in this particular circumstance, and others that might come up similar to this one is simply close your eyes. Then, you will be able to see where they're holding Greg. We'll merely zap Greg directly back here instead of challenging the spirit men. It's not the right time to confront the evil beings."

Frankie did as he was told. He closed his eyes and immediately he saw his brother and three men sitting in a circle on the floor of a cave. They weren't talking or doing anything. Greg and the three spirit men simply sat staring at one another. In the next split second Frankie opened his eyes and Greg was standing right next to him. He closed his eyes again to see how the spirit men reacted when they saw Greg was no longer sitting in the midst of their little circle. The spirit men acted bewildered. They were talking a mile a minute.

Frankie spoiled the fun the spirits were going to have at Greg's expense.

Frankie hugged his brother and said, "I was so worried when I came back and you weren't here. I got flustered and didn't experiment with the powers to see the force I should have used to find you. I had to ask IAM to help me. I'm so sorry I left you alone. I should have taken you with me."

Greg said, Frankie, "Don't worry about it. I figured nothing would happen to me with you nearby."

Frankie asked Greg, "Were you afraid?"

Greg said, "It's a funny thing. I wasn't afraid. I was ticked off that they forced me to go with them, but they didn't hurt me. I could have licked one man at a time but I couldn't fight all three. At first they grilled me with questions pertaining to you, Frankie. I gave them the silent treatment and wouldn't say a word. And then, they stopped talking too. It was so uncanny. We just sat there, staring at one another like we were waiting for something to occur. Their eyes were not the eyes of a fisherman. They were more like the eyes of a hunter."

Greg went on to say, "Frankie, do you recall the way I always used to talk about our eyes being the mirror to our feelings and we could read people merely by looking straight into their eyes? Our eyes show when were happy, sad, frightened and every other emotion we have. I stared straight into the men's eyes. They not only looked like the eyes of a hunter, they looked cold, and calculating, and they were filled with hate. They resembled snake eyes."

Frankie said, "The important thing right now is that you're safe. I want you to meet my friend IAM, the source of my powerful force."

IAM said, "Hello Greg. I'm pleased to meet you. You're a brave soul. The moment for a formal acquaintance with me has to be completed at just the right time and tonight is your time."

Greg said, "I'm pleased to finally meet you. I must admit I'm a bit overwhelmed too. I'm very glad you're on the Stargazer's side."

IAM replied, "Greg, It is the other way around. I am glad you're on my side and pleased that you are. We shall meet again one day."

Then IAM spoke to Frankie saying, "My boy, I'll talk with you again real soon."

Both Stargazer boys said, "Thank you IAM. Good-bye for now."

Directly after they uttered their last words to IAM they found themselves sitting in Frankie's apartment.

Frankie said, "Greg, it's so late and we are both so tired, why don't you just spend the night here?"

In a whisper Greg said, "Okay Frankie. That would be swell. I'm tired and I'm pumped at the same time. I probably couldn't sleep a wink after all the excitement. I never expected our adventure to turn out quite like it did. I don't know how you keep up with everything. You're such a whiz kid. I have to admit sometimes I wonder about all the things you're into and that you're capable of doing."

Frankie said, "So do I Greg, so do I. Surely you must know there are many times I get overwhelmed too."

Greg responded, "Yes, Frankie, I'm aware that everything you do has to be incredibly awesome to you to. What did you think about Planet Purpling?"

Frankie replied, "I thought Planet Purpling was the greatest. I loved seeing the animals grazing, and lazing around together with every breed of animal imaginable. And some of them were unimaginable. I couldn't begin to describe how it felt to sit besides tigers and lions and pet them as if they were kittens. Just think if

Trinka wasn't pulling our leg, then there really is an Animal Heaven."

They both remarked about the way they thought animals died and that was the end of them.

Greg said, " I think it's cool, God in his infinite wisdom gave animals an eternal resting place too. Imagine, what all the different religious denominations would say if we told them about our adventures and all the things we learned and experienced in the last year? We'd probably be called heretics and placed in a home way out in the boonies. They'd put us under lock and key in a rubber room and probably throw the keys away."

The boy's giggled and carried on until they changed the subject and started to talk about their experience in the forest.

Greg got a somber look in his eyes as he said, "Frankie, I need to talk seriously for a minute. You know, after you rescued me in the forest, I had the eerie feeling you knew who those three men were that were holding me hostage in the cave. Tell me about them? I can take it. For goodness sakes, I'm not a child anymore. I'm stronger than you give me credit for. Besides, I'm older than you are Frankie. So talk to me baby brother. Tell me what really happened tonight?"

In a low voice, Frankie said, "I hesitate to talk about certain things. There are some situations that are not only hard for me to talk about but they are hard for me to understand. I'm in the midst of the battle seeing things that no one else sees. I'm afraid discussing what really happened tonight will be too much for you to deal with."

Greg remarked, "Give me a break and tell me. I can handle it. If I can't handle it, I won't tell you. I'll simply jump out the window for a dime like Sam once did."

Frankie said, "Come on Greg, quit being funny. This is serious and mind-boggling."

Greg replied, "All right brother. I'll stop clowning around. Tell me, who in god's creation were those men."

Frankie said, "Okay I'll tell you but if I see you can't take it I'll stop telling you the whole story. What would you think if I told you I could see into some kind of a spirit world? The beings are called spirit men. At first glance the spirits look like they might be friendly, but they are indeed evil and wicked. They're not ugly or ogre looking characters. Except for their eyes. They're handsome and they look like humans. One spirit in particular dresses in a white suit with a gold sash. The others dress in red suits with a gold sash.

"On the way home from Planet Purpling I encountered a few spirits flying toward the earth. I decided to follow them. I probably shouldn't have done that since you were with me. I was responsible for your well-being. I felt like I put you in harm's way, especially when I got flustered and didn't exactly know how to look for you even with X-ray vision. Sometimes I experiment with the powers to find out what I'm capable of performing in any given situation that calls for quick action. Tonight, I found out that I'm vulnerable, even with forces I've been endowed with to rescue people. That's when I called on IAM to help me. He showed me how to use my eyes in yet another way that allowed me to find you.

"The three men you sat in the midst of were not human beings, they were wicked spirit men. They manifested themselves visible and made their appearance look human in order to deceive and use you to get to me. I didn't pick up on the fact that they detected me in space and as I landed in the forest. I was vulnerable twice in the same night. I recognized the need to know more about the abilities I was born with. I need to learn to detect a susceptible situation without endangering anyone, including myself.

"I couldn't exactly detect if they could see me flying because they act like they don't see me. Tonight, I found that they only pretended not to see me flying right next to them. I was taunting them and they ignored me. Whenever the spirits see me fighting crime and turmoil they immediately disappear.

"I'm aware this whole thing sounds far fetched like something out of a science fiction comic book, but it's real. I've been appointed to combat wicked evil spirit beings that constantly enact wrecking havoc. What do you think now, Greg?"

Greg replied, "I don't know much about evil spirits. On the other hand, I do know you, Frankie. I know you would never make up a story of this magnitude. I can't comprehend all you've told me. But I don't doubt your words. Tonight, I witnessed what the spirits are capable of. I had no idea they weren't really people or I might have been fearful and spooked. I simply believed my brother was going to knock their heads together and rescue me at any moment. That sustained me throughout the ordeal of being forced to do something I didn't want to. I picked up on the way they were only interested in you by the kind of questions they asked. I thought you might have prevented them from robbing a bank or something like that.

"I think we should get some books from the library on evil spirits to learn all we can on the subject. Along with the powers you're gifted with, a force fighter should know his enemy and everything he's up against before he goes into battle. We not only need to read library books about evil, we need to read what the Bible say's about evil and evil beings too."

"One Sunday morning during church I was bored with the sermon. While the pastor droned on, I started reading the Bible. The chapter I was reading spoke of Satan and evil spirits. Later on, I asked one of my Sunday school teachers if Satan was real or simply make believe. The teacher pooh-poohed me and never did answer my question."

Frankie said, "You're absolutely right. Greg, there are so many times you amaze me. I do need to read books on the subject. I overlooked the fact that whenever you're unsure and don't know something about a subject the first thing you do is find a book and learn all you can on the subject. You're the scholar in the family. Help me learn as much as I can so I'll be better prepared in my mind as well as in my abilities. We've had quite a night but before we go to sleep, would you mind if I changed the subject. I'd like to know how you really feel toward Melinda?"

"I like Melinda a lot. She is the most beautiful woman I've ever seen. I'd like to get to know her better. I realize it's an impossible situation, but I can dream, can't I?" Greg said.

Frankie said, "I'm relieved that you know being with Melinda is unattainable. It's not like she lives in another state and you could communicate on the telephone or drive somewhere to see her. She's on another planet no one even knows exists. There's no way to correspond with Melinda. Even if you could communicate with her on a regular basis, you're from two very different worlds."

Greg said, "I believe in miracles and that's exactly what it will take to be with Melinda. I know you're worried about me, but you don't have too. I told you once tonight, I'm a big boy now."

Yawning sleepily, Frankie said, "Oky doky. I'm really tired. I can hardly keep my eyes open much longer. Lets get some shuteye."

Greg said, "I was so excited that I didn't think I'd be able to sleep, but I feel exhausted after all. Good-night Frankie."

"Good-night Greg."

Giggling silently, they both said, "Goodnight Kylee dog.

CHAPTER 15...
ANOTHER TIME, ANOTHER PLACE

The next morning Frankie woke up to the sound of someone knocking on the door. Sleepily, he asked, "Who is it?"

"It's me, Joe. Open the door."

Frankie got out of bed and opened the door. Befuddled, he asked Joe. "What are you doing here so early?"

Joe said, "Did you forget about the plans we made for today?"

"Oh golly. I guess I did forget, what were they?" Frankie asked.

Joe replied, "We were going to pick up Greg and drive into the city to spend the day together. You know, just kick back and relax. Maybe take in a movie."

Frankie said, "We don't have to pick Greg up. He spent the night here. I'll wake him up. Give us a few minutes to get dressed."

Frankie woke Greg up. Before to long they were ready to greet the day.

They were driving down the road singing and clowning around when out of the blue, Frankie said, "You know what guys? I can't go with you. There's something I have to do that can't wait."

Joe asked. "What is it, Frankie? Why did you get so serious all of a sudden?"

Frankie sighed, "I can't concentrate on anything until I take care of some unfinished business. I need to talk to IAM."

Joe asked, "Couldn't it wait just one more day? This is the first time in over a year the three of us have been together, just to play around and have fun."

Frankie said, "Tell you what I'll do. I'll take care of business and meet you both at the theatre for the last matinee of the day. We can have a late supper after the movie. Afterwards, we can have an old-fashioned slumber party. We could have a pillow fight and stay up all night long and tease each other."

Joe said, "All right Frankie. You're being so persistent. It must be important."

"Thanks brothers. I'll make it up to you. See you guy's later." Frankie said.

They were driving Frankie's convertible down the highway with the top down. So it was convenient for Frankie to say adios amigo's as he flew right out of the car out into the wild blue yonder.

Frankie wasn't sure why, without any warning, he suddenly felt an urgency to see IAM right away. He didn't whiz by the planets and stars as fast as he usually did. He took his time and savored the sights in the dark beauty of outer space. Taking in the awesome wonders of the moon and the lights from the illuminating clusters of stars, paths of Milky Ways, different colored planets, beautiful rings circling planets like diamonds and crystallized ice. At last Frankie came to Rainbow Star. He landed smack dab in the center of the dazzling, dancing colors.

Before Frankie called out to IAM, he sat on Rainbow Star meditating and basking in the sheer wonder of all that happened through out his childhood.

After what seemed like a very long time Frankie said, "Hello IAM, I need to talk to you."

IAM'S voice called out, "I'm here." For the first time since they began to communicate, Frankie perceived something he'd never heard before. It was the sound of IAM laughing heartily.

Frankie said, "IAM, I want to thank you for the wonderful privileged opportunity you gave me to know you and for appointing me a destiny as awesome as all get out. I love being here. It's so peaceful and refreshing. When I'm flying and sitting on this beautiful star the cares of the world seem like a thing of the past. I wish I never had to go back to earth.

"I feel completely content when I'm here. Nothing else seems to matter. Sure, I'd miss my family and Cynthia something fierce. When I'm here talking to you, even they seem distant and far away. Sometimes it's confusing to love my family and Cynthia more than anything else in the world. Yet, my heart desires to be as close as I can be to your presence."

IAM said, "Frankie, It's perfectly all right to feel the way you do. You know there are different forms of love. You love me in a different way than you love your family. You love me for who I am, and for what I mean to you. You love your family and Cynthia for who they are, and for what they mean to you."

Frankie sighed as he replied, "IAM, I experienced an urgency to hear you're voice and talk to you. I don't exactly know why I felt so anxious. I know I can talk with you anytime I want to. Nevertheless, today, I felt like I was going to burst if I didn't fly to Rainbow Star. It doesn't matter I can't see your form or that I don't know who you are. Just to feel your presence and hear your voice is enough. On the journey here, I wanted nothing more in my life than to bask in the splendor of the Universe. The second the colors of the star came into view, I wanted to ask you if I could stay here forever and ever, for all eternity."

IAM said, "Someday your wish to be with me will come to pass. That day is not today. To every season there is a reason and a time. There is a plan for every man. It's time for all of mankind to let go of the world they know and get ready for the things to come. Time is of the essence for time is running out.

"There will come a day, every one will be judged based on his or her behavior. People have the opportunity to choose whom they will serve. Whether or not they choose to do good or choose to do evil is up to them. Let me put that in another perspective that may be easier for you to understand. It's like this, Frankie. Light doesn't mix with darkness. When you turn a light switch on in a dark room, the darkness that was in the room disappears instantly. When a person walks in the light, there is no way they can walk in darkness at the same time.

"No matter what people believe, their beliefs won't save them. Some people think it's okay to have no standards or morals, and they can walk in darkness and behave in an evil manner. Some estimate it's okay to do nothing to help those in need. Some believe they can worship a chicken or a cow or whatever strange god they have been led to believe in. Every single one of them believes they will categorically have a place in the kingdom of heaven no matter what their belief is. That simply is not true.

"Then, there are those that trust in nothing more than their own self. They suppose that they will be satisfied and rewarded for their misconception. People think many different things for many different reasons. What is most important and what really matters is the decision people make within their own heart.

"If people chose good, they could not and would not commit wicked deeds. There is absolutely no way they would or could believe the myth that says a person can do whatever they want to do and they will still receive a crown of glory and sing praises to the 'Most High God.'

"You see Frankie, you're not the only person in the world with a destiny. Every single individual has a destiny, no matter what they choose. No matter who the individual is or is not, or if they have riches or don't have riches. Everyone does have power. It's called the power to make decisions and pick whom or what they will choose to guide their footsteps.

"There are only two choices that a human has to decide on in the entire Universe. Those two choices are to choose either good or evil. Meaning God or Satan."

Frankie was quiet as he contemplated all the words IAM spoke. After what seemed like a very long time, Frankie said, "IAM, I'll ponder on all the things you've taught me today. It's too much to think about all at one time. On a different note. I'd like to know what you think about my upcoming marriage to Cynthia Butler?"

IAM said, "It's wonderful. Cynthia is the girl of your dreams. You've been in love with her most of your life. She is one of the selected, not only by you son, but by me too. You didn't need my permission to marry Cynthia. However, you do have my blessing. Marriage is more than taking a vow. It is a covenant between God, man and woman."

Frankie replied, "I don't know how much I should reveal about my destiny and my powers to Cynthia."

IAM answered, "You must trust in Cynthia's love. Don't be afraid to reveal you're powers and you're destiny to her. You need to prepare her for the future that you're going to share together."

IAM went on to say, "I'm going to tell you a story about the life of the soldier's in the Old Testament. When a soldier marries, he stays out of battle for a year. He spends that year getting to know his new bride. She in turn learns to know her husband. Frankie, that's what I shall require of you. You're to take a year off and spend the whole time with your new wife.

"That year belongs strictly to you and your wife as the two of you become as one. When the year is over, you're going to encounter battle skirmishes and crusades you never dreamed possible. You're not to worry about anything. I will be right there in the midst of the battle fighting with you. Just enjoy the new beginning you're about to experience in holy matrimony with Cynthia.

"One more thing, it delights and pleasures me to give you and your new bride a furnished house on planet Moonazer. I placed another gift in your apartment. On the day of your wedding, I'm requesting that both you and Cynthia unwrap the gift together. Now son, it's time for you to depart. Go and be happy with the new adventure you're about to embark on with your new bride."

Frankie was overwhelmed with IAM'S generosity. Before he could say thank you, IAM zapped him back to earth.

Once again, Frankie was amazed to find himself back on earth within a split second. There he was, standing in front of the theater with his two brothers.

Joe said, "Frankie, I don't think we will ever get used to your departures and appearances. I hope all went well with your visit. Now that you're here, let's party."

Joe, Greg, and Frankie enjoyed the rest of the day together. It was late in the evening when they finally reached Frankie's apartment. The first thing they noticed when they walked in the door was the box IAM had placed in the middle of the room. It was wrapped in dazzling rainbow colored paper and ribbons.

Joe asked, "What 's in the package?"

Frankie replied, "It is a wedding gift from IAM. I can't open it until my wedding day. Listen guys, are we through having fun. I need to call my bride to be."

Joe and Greg both said, "Yes dear brother, we've had enough bonding time for one day."

Frankie called Cynthia and said, "Hi honey, we just got home. I was wondering if I could pick you up for breakfast at around five-thirty a.m. tomorrow morning?"

Cynthia said, "Okay, mystery man! I'll see you then."

Frankie told his brothers he was much too tired to have a gabfest but they were still welcome to spend the night.

Joe and Greg were tired too so they all decided to go to bed. Frankie set the alarm for five a.m. and in a matter of minutes all three of them were sound asleep.

The next morning, Frankie shut off the alarm and quietly groomed so he wouldn't wake his brothers up. He put the ring Matthew made for Cynthia in his pocket and went to pick up his woman. Cynthia was waiting on the porch. The moment she saw his car pull up, she skipped down the stairs, got in the car and she said, "What's up, Frankie? To what do I owe for the honor of seeing you so bright and early?"

Frankie said, "You'll just have to wait a few more minutes. I'll tell you when were sitting in the diner."

After they arrived at their destination and were seated at a table near the window Frankie took out the ring box and handed it to Cynthia. She opened the little box and tears welled up in her eyes.

She said, "Oh my gosh! This ring is too beautiful for words. Where in the world did you find such a priceless, precious treasure?"

Frankie took the ring out of the box and placed it on her finger saying, "That's for me to know and for you to find out. Maybe one day soon I'll introduce you to the friend that designed and made the ring especially for her."

She exclaimed, "Frankie, I thank you with all my heart." Then she kissed him right then and there in front of everyone in the diner.

Frankie stood up and said, "Hey everyone! I just gave my girl an engagement ring."

Everyone shouted congratulations and clapped their hands for the young couple.

After they ate a hearty breakfast, Frankie took Cynthia for a drive and parked by the lake. Starting with the night he had seen the shooting star that didn't die out, Frankie explained to Cynthia about IAM and all the things that occurred through out the years. He told her about his predestined powers and the awesome tasks he would be performing after they spend an entire year together just getting to know one another.

The fact that Cynthia simply accepted the things Frankie told her without question was amazing. Some how she just knew every word he spoke was true beyond the shadow of a doubt. Even when he told Cynthia they would be staying on another planet called Moonazer for a year, she acknowledged all he said. Cynthia made an oath never to reveal anything her fiancé confided to her.

The months passed quickly and the big day finally arrived. The chapel was adorned in the stunning rainbow colors that became a symbol of Frankie's life. He stood in front of the church bedazzled by his bride as she walked down the aisle with her father.

Cynthia was the most beautiful bride. She fashioned ribbons in her white wedding veil to match the colored stones in her ring. The bride looked like a fragile china doll. Her green eyes sparkled. Cynthia's lovely black hair was piled high on her head and fashioned with curls around her face.

Frankie stood by her side, a most handsome groom with his blond hair slicked down and his blue eyes shining ever so brilliantly. As they took their vows uniting them in holy matrimony, everyone in the church oohed and awed at each word the striking nineteen-year-old couple spoke of in their undying love for one another.

The only time a completely quiet hush came over the people during the wedding ceremony was when Frankie looked straight into Cynthia's radiant eyes while he played his guitar and sang her a new love song that he wrote especially for her. Neither one of their parents could hold back the tears of joy that flowed down their cheeks throughout the service. It wasn't long before the pastor said. "I now pronounce you man and wife." Then turning to everyone in the church he said, "I now present to the world, Mr. and Mrs. Stargazer."

During the reception that was held in the church fellowship room, Frankie took the microphone and said, "Everyone, can I have your attention please? Cynthia and I want to thank you all for attending the happiest day of our lives. WE have a long way to go to our secret honeymoon rendezvous so we're leaving now. Thanks for everything, family and friends. As Cynthia and Frankie are making their way toward the door to leave, Dad Stargazer stops them.

With a worried look on his face Frankie's dad said, "Son will you and Cynthia change you're mind and tell us where you're going? Give me something to go on before you leave. You're mother and the Butler's are beside themselves worrying and wondering what the two of you could possibly be thinking to be gone a whole year without a word from either one of you."

Frankie said, "Dad, we went over this before. I told you Cynthia and I will be all right. You and Mom can rely on Joe and Greg is something comes up. A year isn't that long. Do you trust me Dad?"

Dad remarked, Yes, I do trust you.

Frankie said, "Than that should be enough. You don't have to worry about us. I assure you, we'll be safe. We are looking forward to going away. Cynthia and I will be in seventh heaven. Comfort Mom and tell her what I just told you.

"When you put it that way there's nothing more to say. God watch over you and Cynthia. I'll look forward to the day your scheduled to come home. Go kiss your mother good-bye, " Dad said.

Frankie and Cynthia kissed their parents good-bye and slipped out the door. They got in the car and drove to Frankie's apartment.

Frankie said, "Make your self comfortable Mrs. Stargazer. I'll be right back. I have to get something out of the closet. It's a gift from IAM. He said we should open it together."

Frankie got the beautifully wrapped gift box and presented it to Cynthia. Then, they opened the gift together. Inside the box was a lamp decorated with the same colors that glow on Rainbow star. The lamp was lit but there was no cord or switch in which to turn the lamp on or off.

There was a note from IAM that said, "The lamp will remain lit all the time. The bulb will never grow dim nor will it ever wear out. It is a symbol and a reminder that I am near. I will neither leave nor ever forsake Mr. & Mrs. Frankie Stargazer. Get ready to take the journey to the new home I've prepared for you on Planet Moonazer. Hold each other's hands, and touch the lamp at the same time."

Instantaneously, Frankie and Cynthia were whisked away to planet Moonazer. They were standing directly in front of the house IAM had prepared for them.

It was the most exquisite house they had ever seen. The house had two stories. It was constructed with small blue and white colored bricks. The window frames were trimmed in a silver gray color. The front porch was decorated in a pale rose color. There was outdoor furniture on the porch that consisted of a marble table and chairs. There were flowers and plants placed in vases from one end of the porch to the other.

There was a lamp lit in the bay window that looked exactly like the lamp IAM gave them for their home on earth. As the lamp illuminated the windows they could see the rooms inside the house were painted gold and white. The house was fully furnished with everything they needed and then some.

Frankie picked up his bride still adorned in her wedding dress. He carried her across the threshold into their new house, and into their new life together as a married couple.

THE END

BRIEF SYNOPSIS OF SEQUEL

Frankie Stargazer 2# titled: "Frankie Stargazer's Ultimate Finale."

There is an appointed time for everything. And there is a time for every event under heaven.

It's time to let go of the world we know and get ready for the things to come as Frankie Stargazer, the awesome force fighter encounters the final ultimate battle to end all battles. There is something strange going on, and no one on earth really knows what it is. No one on earth could even venture to guess...except for Frankie Stargazer. The answer to evil will elude the wicked.

Although the story is an adventurous fantasy the text is intertwined with some truths depicting intriguing foresight into what could be the future of mankind.

As time went by, more of the evil-beings living on the dreaded Black Planet are circling and invading earth, wrecking devastating chaos and crime on human beings in record numbers.

Frankie Stargazer's Ultimate Finale attracts attention to family situations, romance, and conflicts that take place between the forces of good and evil. The story culminates into the end of time, as we know it, and the beginning of a new time where the will no longer be any sadness, crying, pain or death.

gunner1@inetnebr.com

Printed in the United States
200376BV00004B/361/A

9 781604 415278